MURDER DOWN THE HILL

A COPPER RIDGE MYSTERY - BOOK 1

AMY GRUNDY

BLUE WHISKERS
PUBLISHING

Copyright © 2019 Amy Grundy
Murder Down the Hill
A Copper Ridge Mystery - Book 1
By Amy Grundy

BLUE WHISKERS
PUBLISHING

ISBN - 978-1-952392-02-3

 Created with Vellum

ACKNOWLEDGMENTS

Special Thanks to:

Gracie Cassias, Beta Reader, and beautiful niece, who sent my first draft to a copy editor, despite my fears... and continued printing and shipping my manuscripts back and forth for every subsequent book, I owe her a lot of postage!

Camille Ingram, Copy Editor - Gotta love the red pen. Just kidding, but if she did use a red pen, I'd probably owe her a whole new box! No matter what color ink, her corrections made my books so much better, for that I thank her.

Sarah Hobbs, Content Editor - In just the short time we've worked together, I have learned a lot. She has the ability to cut through a clunky sentence and make it clear. Writers, if you need a content editor, you could not go wrong with Sarah.

And **Daniela Colleo**, Cover Artist - Thank you so much for your patience. I know I am very picky! If anyone needs a really Stunning Book Cover, she made it so easy for a first time author.

To my loving husband, David.
Without you this would have never happened.
You make me smile everyday.

CHAPTER ONE

I TURNED AROUND HOLDING my favorite, an iced caramel latte, and immediately felt the cold liquid splash down my shirt. I jumped back, pulling the bottom of my soggy T-shirt away from my skin.

"Oh, my gosh, I'm so sorry. Here, let me help you."

I watched as the blonde stranger tried to pat my coffee-soaked shirt dry. "I can't believe I did that, I'm not usually such a klutz."

"It's ok, I didn't need all that caffeine anyway." I laughed trying to put her at ease.

She handed me a wad of napkins. "Hi, I'm Maggie, please forgive me. I sure didn't mean to run into you."

The barista made me a new coffee in a matter of moments and Maggie held it out to me. She appeared to be about my age, blue eyes, blonde bob cut to her chin and a warm engaging smile.

"I'm Emily," I introduced myself to her, "Glad to meet you, and don't worry about it, accidents happen. It's a really old T-shirt and it'll wash off anyway." We walked out of the coffee shop together.

"Are you new in town?"

"Yes, as a matter of fact, I am, I just moved here. I was actually taking a break from cleaning. I bought that little Craftsman, think I heard it was the old Weston house a few streets over."

"Oh, I know that house. It's been vacant for a while," she said with a hesitant look on her face.

"Yes, that's the one alright. I think I might have bit off a little more than I can chew with that house."

"What do you mean?"

"I knew I'd have to hire someone when I was ready to do any major renovations, but when I initially saw it, I didn't realize the amount of work it was actually going to need. I'm trying hard not to feel overwhelmed."

A broad grin spread across her face. "How would you like an extra pair of hands? Don't mean to brag, but I did a really good job refurbishing my place." Maggie pointed down the street. "That's my florist shop right there and I live above it. I did the demolition in preparation for having the kitchen built, did all the painting, put in the tile and refinished the old hardwood floors."

"Wow," I was impressed, "but no, we've just met. I wouldn't think of asking you to help." I paused, "I'll be okay." I'm sure she sensed my hesitation.

"How about this, why don't I come over? I can take a look around and give you some pointers. How does that sound?"

"Like a godsend," I admitted. "Thank you." We decided to meet up again the next day, and in the meantime, I and my coffee-stained T-shirt would go shopping for paint.

CHAPTER TWO

"OKAY, today is going to be a productive day," I told myself, climbing out of bed. I stretched, trying to loosen up the tight muscles in my back. I thought I was in pretty good shape, but my sore arms and back were telling me differently. I put on a pot of coffee and tied back my dark red hair. I taped off the baseboards in the living room the night before and pulled out a new can of paint. I had made a killing on the old small Craftsman bungalow which had been vacant and on the market for a couple of years. I had fallen in love with the interior wood beams and trim. After some cleaning, they revealed their rich red chestnut stain. There were built-in bookshelves in the living room on either side of the fireplace with small rectangular stained-glass windows above each of them. The realtor convinced me the house just needed a little elbow grease, and I convinced myself that it was true. It would be an understatement to say home repair had ever been my strong suit, but it was too late to turn back now. Before I could even pour the paint, I heard a knock at the door. Who the heck would be knocking at my door at this time of the morning?

"Knock, knock," I heard someone calling out.

I opened the door to see Maggie's smiling face.

"Boy, you're up early," I grinned at her.

"I know, and even better, I brought goodies." She held up a white bag. "Have you been to The Little Copper Cafe yet?"

"Oh yes." I laughed, "Is that something Claudette baked?" My mouth began to water at the thought of what could be in that white bag. Everything Claudette baked was tasty; she had a real gift.

"Yep, and since I didn't know your preference, I brought a variety, orange cranberry bread, and brown sugar cinnamon scones."

"Yum, come on in. I just put the coffee on."

"Here, you take the goodies and let me go get a few things out of the car."

Maggie made a couple of trips back and forth, it looked like she came equipped with everything, including her toolbox, stepstool, drop cloths, paint roller, and brushes.

"Wow, it looks like you've done this before."

"Told you," she grinned.

We sat down together at my kitchen table to have our breakfast and picked up a conversation together like we were old friends.

"So how do you like Copper Ridge so far?"

"Well, I haven't been here very long, but I needed a change and a new start. I fell in love with Copper Ridge the first time I visited, and it seems like a good place to get that start. You see, my mom recently passed away. She was the only family I had."

"Oh, Emily, I'm sorry to hear that." Maggie's face showed genuine concern.

"And it gets a little worse, I had been in a relationship

for a couple of years. I thought he was a good guy. In fact, I thought he was the one, but when Mom got sick, I saw a whole new side of him. It seems like my family wasn't important to him, and I just knew we were done. He was a complete jerk. I know that now, but I have to admit, the loss still stings a bit."

"That's a lot of grief and upheaval all at one time." Maggie reached over to give my hand a pat. "I'm sorry about your mother. I know it's awful losing someone that close to you. I was raised here mostly by my grandpa and grandma. My grandma passed away a couple of years ago and I still feel that pain." She paused for a moment, "Copper Ridge is a great small town and I'm glad you're here. I think you'll really like it."

I looked up, giving her a grateful smile.

She stood up from the table taking a final sip of coffee, "Okay, enough of the serious business. Tell me, what's the plan for today?"

"Well, I had planned on painting. Here, let me show you around." I hopped up and gave her a tour of my new little home. "I just had the bathroom redone, and I love how it turned out, but I'm not sure I want the same company working on the kitchen. I thought they were a little pricey and not as dependable as I would have liked."

"I love the black detail trim and those little white hexagon tiles. And that clawfoot tub! I'm jealous."

"Yes, I've always wanted one of those. Kind of partial to relaxing in a hot tub after I run. By any chance are you a runner?"

Maggie laughed out loud, "Ah, heck no, not unless I'm being chased by a bear and we don't have bears here in town."

I laughed, "You never know, it's kind of fun."

"Well, my idea of fun is a good movie, a walk on a sandy beach or getting my hair and nails done, or even gutting a kitchen for that matter."

I gave her a smile, "Who knows, you might get your chance to have fun in my kitchen then, just not right away. Thought I'd eventually get someone in to redo the kitchen floor and countertops, maybe a new sink. I'd love one of those farmhouse sinks, but for now, I can use it the way it is. As for the rest of the house, I figured I could do the painting myself, but I'm not sure about redoing these floors though. I also need to get some new light fixtures put up, which I definitely know I can't do."

"I can probably help you with the new lights, getting them up isn't as bad as you would think. Ready to get started?"

"Are you always this energetic?" I laughed. "Don't get me wrong, I'm grateful you are here and I know I need all the help I can get with this house."

"Ha! You'll get used to me. Now show me what color you planned to paint this living room."

I opened the can of paint, revealing a creamy antique off-white color. I chose this for the living room and dining room. "I'm not the best at picking paint colors. Do you think this will look good?"

"I think it'll be perfect," Maggie responded. "You can incorporate color if you wanted with accent pieces."

We spent the morning talking, laughing and painting. It was so much better doing this work with a friend and it looked like I had found a good one in Maggie, even if she didn't like running. I practically shuddered at the thought of getting my hair and nails done. My hair was long, straight and naturally red. I only went in periodically to get my bangs and ends trimmed. I had never had a professional manicure in my whole life. Maggie seemed to read my mind.

"So now that we have had fun painting, next time we can have fun getting a manicure."

I just shook my head and laughed. "We'll see."

CHAPTER THREE

I GRABBED my jacket and headed out the door. The skies were clear, the moon full, and the scent of pine hung in the air. Evenings like this made me miss my mom. We had enjoyed short walks together in the evenings while she was still able. Mom always encouraged me to be independent and think for myself, so with a good inheritance, and memories of a mother who loved me, I decided to make a change and launch my business.

Copper Ridge was an old historic town at the base of the Angel Mountains. At one time, there had been an active copper mine, up on the mountain, but it had long since closed. The town had endured economic ups and downs; currently, it was supported mainly by tourism. People came to hike, raft and explore the shops owned by local artisans.

Copper Ridge was also the home of the famous Gage Hotel. It was an old hotel, built back in the 1800s, and was said to be haunted. I came to the town for a visit before moving here and fell in love with the town and scenery. It was the perfect place to start my new business, hosting a combination of historical and ghost tours. I wasn't sure I believed in ghosts, but I loved history and telling stories, and I also enjoyed meeting new people. Coupled with an old historic town, I hoped that I had a winning combination.

I showed up at the old Gage Hotel early. Gazing up at the hotel, I thought to myself that it was magnificent.

This was going to be the starting point for all my tours due to the generosity of its current owners, Mr. and Mrs. Horner. In exchange for a little free publicity, the Horner's would provide a ticket for each guest to enjoy a complimentary drink at their bar after each tour.

I waited for my guests outside by one of the wrought iron benches. It was going to be a small group tonight, but since it was my first tour, I was okay with that. I was a little apprehensive, I really should have done more studying before this tour. But it was too late now. A few minutes later two ladies walked up.

"Good evening, ladies, are you here for the ghost tour?"

"Yes," one of them said. "I'm Pam and this is my friend Donna. We have another couple of ladies coming with us, they said they'd be just a moment."

"No worries, we will wait right here and get started when they show up. Are you ladies from around here?"

"No, we came in to do some shopping, browse the antiques, and check out the quilt shops."

About that time the other two ladies arrived. "Sorry, we didn't mean to keep you waiting," they said.

"No problem, it's just going to be the five of us tonight. My name is Emily Rose, and I'll be your tour guide tonight." I smiled to myself. Whoever thought I'd have my own business? The other ladies introduced themselves as Rita and Carla.

"Let's get started," I suggested. "This is the Gage Hotel. It was built back in the 1800s by Mr. Horatio Randolph

Gage. It was the largest building in the little town when it opened."

The hotel is a three-story building with a limestone exterior. There was a long balcony on the second floor that ran the front length of the building, providing cover to the entrance and the front of the building. The balcony was edged and supported with wrought iron railing and posts. "The current owners are Mr. and Mrs. Horner. The hotel has been remodeled over the years, but currently, it is the best of both worlds. It has been restored to bring back the old charm and brought up to date to include all the modern conveniences. It is now one of the most desirable historic hotels in the area."

The ladies gazed up at the hotel, admiring the exterior. As we entered the hotel, their eyes lit up.

"I think next time we come to town we need to stay here," Pam exclaimed, clearly admiring the hotel's interior. The floors were tile down the middle of the hotel lobby with dark hardwood floors off to each side. The ceilings were gold-stamped tin panels, interspersed with large, dark wooden beams. There were huge chandeliers hanging in the lobby and luxurious arrangements of flowers scattered throughout.

"We could, but there'd go my shopping money," Donna commented.

"As the story goes, ladies, multiple guests reported seeing a man dressed in a suit which makes him appear to be from the 1800s."

"Well, I wonder who he was and what he wants?" Carla asked looking at me with an excited look on her face.

"It is said he can be seen walking up and down various corridors of the hotel as if he is looking for some-thing or someone." I thought to myself, I was going to have to do better than that. I was going to need to do some research.

I put on my best creepy voice, "That's all he appears to do. Walking the corridors of the hotel, searching, always searching for someone."

We made our way to the courthouse in the town square and walked around it. I relayed stories regarding the building of the courthouse as best I could. Then we headed over to the old jail.

"This is the old town jail, also built in the 1800s, not too long after the town was founded. As you can see it's a relatively small stone building. Back in the day, ladies, if you were married to the jailer, your home might have been upstairs in this very building."

This spurred several comments from all the ladies. "Oh, I don't think so," said Pam, "it's so small".

"Not to mention the criminal element," Rita commented.

"So, any ghosts at this jail?" Carla asked.

I knew of none, but I thought quickly. "Well, there are multiple reports of people hearing the clanking of chains and the occasional slamming of the cell doors. Unfortunately, we can't get into the jail, but maybe that's a good thing." I laughed.

We climbed the hill and ended our tour that evening at the town's original cemetery.

"This is the first cemetery the town had. You can see how worn some of the headstones are. If you look around you'll see some of these graves date back to the 1800s, including those of the town founders. Feel free to take some time to walk around." Pam, Donna, and Carla walked through the cemetery, looking at the various old headstones. Rita stayed with me, "I'm not walking through there," she laughed nervously, "Something may reach out and grab me!"

I laughed, "It's ok, Rita, I'll keep you safe."

After the other three ladies finished their stroll through the darkened cemetery, we started back down the hill. We stopped outside the Gage Hotel. "I hope you enjoyed your evening, ladies," I said, as I started to hand out drink tickets.

"Maybe we can take the tour again next time we're in town. I want to see some ghosts." Carla declared.

"Carla! There's no such things as ghosts," Rita laughed, as she took her drink ticket from me.

"Oh, I saw you standing at the gate of the cemetery with Emily, ya big chicken!" Carla teased her good-naturedly.

Donna stood there and watched the exchange between the two. "Don't mind them, they're like this all the time."

"No worries." I smiled watching the interaction between the ladies.

"Thanks, Emily, we had fun," Pam shook my hand. "Come on children," I watched Pam and Donna herd their other two friends toward the hotel.

"Good night ladies," I called, "Enjoy the rest of your evening, and watch out for Mr. Gage."

Well, my first tour was done, and it showed how lacking I was. I needed to do some more research about the town. I'm sure it had a fascinating history and I needed to make better use of it. I definitely had a lot of room for improvement, but I knew I could get better.

CHAPTER FOUR

THE MORNING DAWNED chilly and a little foggy, but it couldn't bring down my spirits. I was finally getting my business off the ground. I had completed my first ghost tour; even though it was done free of charge, it was worth getting some practice in. It had a few rocky moments, but the ladies seemed to have enjoyed it. I headed out the door feeling like I was on top of the world. I loved the fog and this morning I decided to walk into town for breakfast. I was on my way to my favorite breakfast spot, The Little Copper Cafe. It was located across the street from the courthouse and the town square.

The little bell rang over the door as I opened it. Claudette, the owner, was pouring coffee behind the counter as I walked in.

"Good morning, Emily," Claudette gave me a wave and smile.

The cafe was warm and homey, smelling of fresh brewed coffee, freshly-baked muffins, and maple-crusted bacon. I loved the smell of breakfast. Claudette was in her late fifties, with soft brown hair and a curvy figure. I knew that she could never replace my mother, but she had gone out of her way to make me feel welcome when I first moved into town.

"Good morning, Claudette, how's it going this morning?" I asked, taking a seat at the counter.

Claudette smiled, pouring me some coffee and moving the creamer closer to my cup. "I heard you had a good crowd last night for your first tour."

"Oh?" I asked, giving her a puzzled look.

"Yes, had the ladies in earlier this morning." She laughed, "They made quite the group. When I had a chance to talk to them, they said they really enjoyed your tour."

I couldn't keep the grin off my face. "It was sort of a practice run, but for the first tour, it went okay. I had some basic information. I'm going to go through the archives at the newspaper so I can get my stories straight. And tomorrow I have an appointment to meet the lady over at the historical society."

"Mrs. Smithers, you mean? She is such a sweetie, you'll enjoy talking to her."

Claudette went on her way, assisting other customers. Between the locals and the tourists, she always seemed to have a good crowd in for breakfast and lunch.

I had placed my order for a blueberry muffin to go with my coffee. It was one of those giant muffins, made with fresh blueberries and crumble topping. I just started sipping my extra creamy cup of coffee when the door opened, bringing in a petite young brunette. Her hair was perfectly curled and she was dressed very fashionably in boots and leather jacket.

Claudette greeted her with a big smile and waved her to

a seat. With limited table seating available, she also took a seat at the counter, looking a little out of place.

"Just coffee for me," she nodded to Claudette.

"Anything else I can get for you?" Claudette asked, pouring her coffee.

"A job," the lady huffed. "I'm sorry, I didn't mean to snap. I had a job lined up with Alan at the paper and now that looks like it's fallen through."

"Well, we are pretty well staffed up here, but I hear Maggie is looking for some part-time help over at her shop. She's our local florist. Her shop is right down the street and she should be opening shortly."

"I'm not sure. I've never had anything to do with plants and flowers before."

"I don't think that's too important right now. From what she said, she is looking for someone to help cover the phones and take orders," Claudette volunteered.

Priscilla's face seemed to brighten up a bit, "Thanks, I'll stop in to see her."

Claudette held her hand out, "My name's Claudette. Tell her I sent you down."

"I'm Priscilla. Thank you, I will," Priscilla said shaking her hand.

Priscilla finished her coffee and left. Afterward, Claudette came by, poured me some more coffee and quietly said, "Not sure who that was, but if Alan over at the paper was willing to give her a shot, she can't be too bad."

"She sure was a sharp dresser. Wonder if she'll be okay with something part-time?" I asked her.

Claudette had to hurry off to take care of another few customers who had walked through the door. She was definitely busy these days.

I finished up my coffee and muffin, paid my check and

got up to leave. I laughed as Claudette came over to me with a small white paper bag. Without looking in it, I assumed it contained a slice of her glazed orange cranberry bread. What could I say? She was thoughtful, and she knew I loved my carbs as well as her baked goods. "You're the best, Claudette," I said, giving her a quick hug.

CHAPTER FIVE

LATER THAT MORNING I ventured back into town to get some research done. I discovered soon after moving to Copper Ridge that I could not learn everything about the town via the Internet. I wanted the most accurate information possible about some of the historical buildings in town, and any of the stories I could get about the people who used to live here. I could embellish ghost stories, but I preferred at least some grain of truth. I laughed to myself, or as much truth as I could have with a ghost story. So, I set off to the paper to go through their archives.

I was greeted at the paper and was led to the microfiche and also shown the way to the archives. After hours of reading and making notes, I decided to take a break. As I approached the break room I could hear voices. I stopped, brought up short by the tension I heard. It sounded like Jillian, one of the reporters here at the Copper Ridge Chronicle. From what I heard, she was born and raised in Copper Ridge. She was young and pretty, with long blonde hair and green eyes. I met her when I first moved into town; she had been doing a story on Claudette's cafe. Jillian called it a "puff piece". She was pleasant during the interview with Claudette, but she was also annoyed that she was never given serious news to write about. She had said she wanted a meaty story, not just stories about the county fairs and church picnics.

Now she sounded angry, and she was having a very heated conversation. Listening closely, I recognized the second voice as Simon, the lead reporter at the paper. Simon was older and had been working at the paper for twenty years or so. His position had also made him a bit arrogant and not at all willing to share any story that had the potential for being something big.

I didn't mean to eavesdrop, but Simon was loud and I heard him saying, "Listen, just face it, I'm better at the real issues and important news. You, my dear, are better at bake sales." I could hear him stomping back down the hallway.

I entered the break room and came face to face with Jillian, her face red with rage. She had angry tears in her eyes. "I will not cry," she said more to herself than me, "but that man gets under my skin. No one takes me seriously," she continued to rant. She walked to the counter and slammed her coffee cup down. She turned back around to face me, "I'm sorry," she said, shaking her head, "I shouldn't let him get to me like that. I apologize for my outburst. That was not very professional of me." She rubbed her forehead as if to ease the tension away.

For the first time since entering the room, I had a chance to speak. "I'm sorry if I interrupted," I stammered, uncertain of exactly what I should say. "It must be rough starting a new job here."

"But I'm not new here," she muttered. "I know, I need to give it some time." She seemed to be getting worked up again. "I've been working here for almost four years now and I still can't get assigned to any serious news stories. What do I get instead? I get assignments about store openings, new babies and quilt groups. Did you know I was the one who discovered the story of Mr. Richards' questionable business dealings? But who got to break the story? Simon, of course! If he thinks he is so good, why not work for a bigger newspaper?"

I still had said very little, thinking to myself that sometimes it's best to let folks vent. When it looked like she was winding down I offered encouragement, "Hang in there, Jillian. You're smart, your time will come." This seemed like lame encouragement, but it was all I could think of. I felt like I could never think of the right thing to say in situations like this.

"Thanks for listening, Emily." She sighed and turned to refill her coffee cup.

I mumbled a weak, "You're welcome." And watched as she walked off back to her desk with her shoulders sagging.

When I finished up at the paper, I knew I'd be back, but it was enough for one day. I stood up and stretched, trying to work the kinks out. I loved this research, but it sure could make me tired. I left the newspaper with no further signs of Simon or Jillian. I decided to stop by the coffee shop and pick myself up a latte as a reward.

CHAPTER SIX

I ORDERED my coffee to go and drank it as I strolled down the street. I loved this time of year. The weather was starting to have a crispness in the air, and the leaves would soon be turning the vibrant shades of yellow, orange and red. I glanced in the flower shop and saw Maggie working on an arrangement and decided to stop in to see her. Her shop, called Maggie's Creations, was a few doors down from The Little Copper Cafe. The calypso blue and white awning covering the entrance and big front window contrasted nicely with the pale seafoam color inside. It was a quaint little shop and she had made good use of the space, with plants and a few bouquets tastefully arranged on wooden crates and tables. Galvanized metal buckets scattered around the room held various types of flowers. Her floral cooler holding roses was set up on the far wall. Despite the rustic feel of the shop, she had put her feminine twist into the design which included a beautiful antique crystal chandelier to supplement the stores other lighting.

"Hey," Maggie called as I entered the shop, "How's it going?"

I took a deep breath; the aroma of the various flowers was so soothing. "What are you working on?" I asked.

"Oh, this arrangement is pretty straightforward, a dozen red roses. Guess who's fighting again? I swear, Simon must be very difficult to live with. I heard Dara had an appointment to see her lawyer. Now look who's sending his wife some roses."

Whatever was going on in town, Maggie seemed to know about it. I had no idea how she always seemed to know so much about everyone else's business. She had grown up in Copper Ridge and seemed to know everyone. She introduced me to her friends and this, in turn, had helped me get a meeting base for my tours.

"Are you finally getting settled?" Maggie asked, as she added a few more sprigs of baby's breath to the arrangement.

"Yes, my living room furniture was delivered."

"Ooh, what did you get?"

"I go for comfort. So, it's a standard upholstered blue-grey couch. Contemporary, but not too modern. I guess you could say, it's something I can lay down on and enjoy a good book on a rainy day. The chair is nice and puffy but doesn't take up too much room. I got mom's dining room table out of storage. It matches the house nicely. And thanks to you, and my floors are looking great. I can't thank you enough for all your help." Besides painting, she had also helped me sand and refinish the hardwood floors. She definitely wasn't afraid of hard work. "I really love how it all turned out."

"Ah, it was my pleasure, anyway, that's what friends are for." She finished up the roses and called her delivery driver. We chatted a few more minutes, agreed to meet for dinner one night that week and I left on my way to pick up some takeout.

The downside of a smaller town was the limited eating options. The upside was what restaurants Copper Ridge had, fancy or not, were excellent. I stopped by Joe's BBQ and picked up a chopped beef sandwich and some of their famous apple cobbler to go. I wanted to go home and get started reviewing all the information I had picked up at the paper.

With all my notes and copies of old newspaper articles all spread out across the table, I dug in. I had several piles, each on different buildings around town. I thought I'd start on the story of Evergreen Manor. This was a large four-story Victorian manor with a limestone exterior, built in the American Queen Anne style. It had twenty rooms and over sixty windows. The house was built in the mid-1800s and owned by the local railroad tycoon. Mr. Armstrong moved his wife and family in. At that time there was not much to the town, but the new Mrs. Armstrong was a strong woman. At least she was until the flu epidemic swept the town. It took the life of her husband and her twin girls, despite the care she had given them. Mrs. Armstrong took sick herself and a maid started taking care of the young baby. Before long the maid became sick herself, tripped and fell down the stairs in the house while carrying the baby. The baby and maid were both killed in the fall. Mrs. Armstrong was left alone. As the story goes she recovered from her illness but was never the same after that. Her whole family was gone and she fell into a deep depression. She lived out her life in solitude. It's said that lights could be seen in the windows late at night, especially in the nursery. Some people believe it's Mrs. Armstrong wandering around the house crying over the loss of her precious family.

Then there was the old Copper Ridge Cemetery, which I knew was the town's first cemetery. It was a bit creepy at night, but I hadn't heard the stories associated with it. According to the information I had found, there were stories about a mining accident that occurred back in the day and some of the miners who died in that accident are buried there. There are some reports of people seeing floating orbs of light in the cemetery, possibly the ghosts of miners carrying their lamps. There are also tales of people hearing what sounds like children laughing. So far, I hadn't been able to find any further information relating to the sounds of children. I'd have to keep researching those claims. But for now, I had some good material to work with.

CHAPTER SEVEN

TODAY, my plan was to make a trip to the historical society to see what other information I could dig up. I woke up late and hurried to get ready. I had an appointment this morning to meet with Mrs. Smithers. She was a white-haired elderly lady who managed the historical society. She was born and raised in Copper Ridge and she knew everyone in the area. Or at least that's what I had heard. In fact, several generations of her family had called Copper Ridge their home, which gave her a little more insight into the town than most people.

The historical society was set up in the old courthouse across from the town square. The courthouse itself was built in the late 1800s, limestone block walls accented with red sandstone and capped with domes and an intricate clock tower. It was four stories, with one side of the ground floor dedicated solely for the use of the historical society.

I walked up the stone steps and into the lobby. Mrs. Smithers came to meet me when I entered.

"Good morning, you must be Emily," she said, extending her hand. She had snowy white hair and bright red lipstick, which on her, looked perfect. As a matter of fact, her makeup looked expertly applied. Large round brightly colored glasses hung around her neck on a beaded chain.

"Yes, thanks for meeting with me."

"No problem, my dear, what can I help you with?"

"I have a new business giving ghost tours and I'd like to find any information I can on some of the old buildings in town."

"Ghosts, you say?" her eyes lighting up. "Well, I might be able to help you there. When you've lived here as long as I have, you sometimes hear things," she paused, "that don't have a proper explanation," she gave me a playful little grin, "if you know what I mean." Why don't we get started?"

She ushered me to one side of the room and walked me through the history of the town shown in displays set up on the walls.

"Mrs. Smithers, what can you tell me about the Carriage House?"

She pulled her glasses off and turned to look at me, "Oh, that's such a lovely old Victorian home. I love those wide porches that wrap around the front and side of the house. You know that stained-glass window on the top floor was custom-made in Italy." She dug through a file and pulled out some old photos of the home taken a couple of years after it was built. "The home was originally owned by the town banker." She gave me a detailed rundown of the property and its history. "Carriage House is now owned by a couple, and I hear they have worked hard to get it restored. It's supposedly very pretty now, although I haven't been inside. I do believe they have turned it into a bed and breakfast."

"Is it haunted?" I asked, teasing her.

She laughed, "Well, honey, if you believe in that sort of thing. There has been some talk. I hear the owners and some guests have reported hearing noises."

"What kind of noises?" I asked with a smile.

"Party noises to be precise. The sounds of people laughing, glasses clinking and even music playing. Maybe it was the recent construction that has stirred up some of the spirits there."

"Maybe they should advertise it as a haunted B&B. They might get more business from those interested in haunted sites."

"Yes, but the owners don't say a lot about it. I'm not sure what they think about owning a haunted B&B."

I spent all morning listening to Mrs. Smithers talk about the town, absorbing every tidbit of information I could.

"Look, my dear, this is a photo of the courthouse when it was first built and the clock before it was installed. And oh, look at this one." She pushed a photo across the counter in my direction, "It's the town square when they were working on it. That gazebo was added later. They built it when I was a little girl." She got a faraway look in her eyes, "I guess that makes it positively ancient," she laughed, with a jolly twinkle in her eyes.

We looked at displays and rummaged through boxes of old musty-smelling papers, and perused through stacks of old photographs of the homes and buildings in Copper Ridge. I browsed through stacks of photos of people, many with haunted looks on their faces. Times had not always been easy in Copper Ridge, especially when the mine closed down. Like any town, it had its ups and downs. I was fascinated, listening to Mrs. Smither's, as she talked to me about the town's history. She had quite the talent for story-telling.

"Mrs. Smithers, thank you so much for your time this morning. I've loved hearing more about our town and its history, especially the way you tell it."

She gave me a big smile, "You're so welcome, my dear. You can come back and visit with me anytime and I'll see what other information I can dig up for you," she said, patting my arm.

"Oh, I'll definitely be back and thanks again," I said.

All this information was going to provide me with more details for my tours. I was right, I had hit the jackpot with this town.

CHAPTER EIGHT

I HURRIED home so I could go over some of the details provided by Mrs. Smithers and the information I had picked up from the newspaper. Tonight would be my second tour and I wanted to see how much of the new information I could incorporate.

It was a good night, although a little breezy, but nothing that would hinder us. I had about six people scheduled for the tour tonight and they all showed up right on time. I took a deep breath, trying to calm myself and started in, hoping I would do better tonight.

"Good evening, all, my name is Emily and I'll be leading you on what I hope will be an eerily entertaining tour tonight. We are going to get started on our tour right here. This is the Gage Hotel." We worked our way through the lobby, small library, and gardens, while I explained the history of the hotel.

We walked back through the hotel, stopping again in the lobby. I turned back to my group, "A few years after this hotel opened, there was a man who suffered a horrendous injury right outside the hotel. He was crossing the road to enter the hotel when he was tragically run down by a team of spooked runaway horses. The victim was brought into the hotel and placed in a room right down that hallway," I motioned pointing to the right. "The town doctor was summoned and tried to save him. Unfortunately, his injuries were too severe and he died later that day. As the story goes the man was coming into the hotel to meet his soon-to-be bride who was waiting for him here. They were to be married that same day. Since then hotel guests have reported seeing a young man, dressed in a period suit, holding his rounded derby hat, walking through the halls. His hair is combed and his mustache is waxed like he was coming to his wedding. Whenever anyone tries to follow him, he disappears around a corner and is gone. He appears to be searching, walking the halls, in the gardens, in the lobby and especially walking the corridor close to room number 120. Some guests have even heard a knocking on their door when staying in that room. The man who died was none other than Mr. Gage, the original owner of the Gage Hotel. He was coming back to the hotel from getting his hair cut. Coming to meet his bride for their wedding. She was staying in room 120. His bride was heartbroken by his untimely death and returned to her family back East. He has been in the hotel searching for her ever since."

One of my guests spoke up, "but I'm staying down that hallway." She had a hesitant look on her face.

One of the young men in my group spoke up, "That's awesome. Maybe you'll be lucky enough to see the ghost of Mr. Gage tonight."

"I'd rather not," was the lady's hurried response.

I looked over at her, "If it makes you feel any better, the ghost of Mr. Gage has never attempted to harm anyone. He just appears to be searching for his lovely bride." She seemed to be a bit reassured by my explanation. And I couldn't help but notice a few grins on my other guest's faces.

After the hotel, we made stops at the courthouse, jail, and the Carriage House.

Our final stop was at the old Copper Ridge Cemetery. We climbed up one of the little hills that overlooked the old downtown. Even though it was dark, there was enough light to see our surroundings. The moon was full, the crickets were chirping, and I could even see the occasional lightning bug. I gave them the historical background for the cemetery and allowed time for the group to look around. As I was waiting for all my guests to meet me back by the front gate, I looked around and thought I saw a shadow. I looked closer and saw what I thought was someone slinking through the trees on the other side of the cemetery fence. Who in the world would be out there, cutting through the woods at this time of night? I shook my head; no one, I thought, it must have been my imagination. I laughed to myself, too many ghost stories.

CHAPTER NINE

THE NEXT DAY as I entered The Little Copper Cafe, I noticed there was quite the buzz in the air. Claudette was busy with a customer, so I took a seat at the counter and waited. I didn't have to wait long before she came over. I was ready to order until I saw the look on her face.

"Have you heard?" she asked.

She seemed a bit agitated. "Heard? Heard what?" thinking I was just wanting my coffee and to get my breakfast ordered. I was still deciding between my favorite orange cranberry bread or to go all out and enjoy some sourdough French toast.

"It's Simon; he's dead, and the word is it didn't look accidental," she whispered hurriedly.

News like that had a way of taking away my appetite. "What?" I was stunned. I had just seen him, more precisely had heard him the day I was at the paper. My brain was spinning. How could something like this happen in Copper Ridge? It seemed like such a quiet little town.

Claudette poured me some coffee and went on to tell me a couple of joggers had found him early this morning. I was thinking to myself it was a good thing I had slept late and missed my run.

Speculation was running wild in the diner. Claudette had no real information, and no one really knew what had happened to him. I couldn't help but think about the fight I had overheard between Simon and Jillian. Or maybe Simon's wife got tired of living with a no-good...I sat sipping my coffee, continuing to mull over the news of Simon's death. My thoughts were interrupted by the delivery of my breakfast. I had settled on a cheese and veggie omelet to go along with my orange cranberry bread. I guess I hadn't lost my appetite after all. As I was eating my breakfast I couldn't help but overhear the other diners and their speculations. A couple at the table behind me were discussing his possible murder, rather loudly.

"Well, it's a wonder he hadn't been targeted sooner. He was a jerk, thinking he knew it all. He sure did know how to make enemies." The man's wife shushed him, telling him to keep his opinions to himself. After all, "It's not good to speak ill of the dead," she said.

I watched his distorted reflection on a mirrored service, her comment prompting a raised eyebrow from her husband. "I know, I know," she said. "He wasn't the easiest to get along with, but he did have some big stories for the paper. You have to give him credit for that." Their topic of conversation changed and I decided I should mind my own business. In the back of my head, though, I couldn't help but wonder what had happened to Simon. Murdered, wow, I still couldn't believe it. Maybe a trip over to the newspaper office was in order. It couldn't hurt and after all, I was in town already.

Claudette came over to refill my coffee cup.

"No more for me Claudette, I'm good thanks. Here you

go," I said as I handed her some cash to pay for my breakfast. "That was really yummy."

"Glad you liked it."

"Of course, I like everything you make here," I laughed. "I also think I need to start running again to work off some of these calories."

"Ah, you're a young thing, you've got nothing to worry about."

I stood up, "I'd better go for now. You have a good day and I'm sure I'll be back in for another meal soon."

She waved good-bye to me as she returned to her work, making rounds around the cafe with her coffee pot.

CHAPTER TEN

I STOPPED by the newspaper after doing a little shopping. I figured I'd take a bit of time for things to calm down over at the paper. When I walked in, there seemed to be an air of stunned silence. I found Jillian in her cubicle, her eyes red from crying. She was making a halfhearted effort to look like she was working.

"Hello, Jillian," I said softly. "I'm so sorry to hear about Simon."

She dropped her head, looking like she was going to start crying again. "We are waiting to hear something from the police," she whispered. "Everyone is saying someone killed him. I know he could be a jerk, and he made enemies from some of the stories he wrote, but I never thought someone would want to kill him."

"Enemies?" I asked.

"Well, yes, he made people angry with his news stories, all the time, especially his last big story. You've probably read it. Remember I was telling you how I had uncovered news about a local businessman with some possible illegal activities. Anyway, Simon got the story on him. His name is

James Richards. He was arrested for allegedly running an illegal gambling ring out of the back of his business and for stealing some money that he was supposed to be investing. He always supported town events and seemed like a good man. He was well-liked. There were threats made by Mr. Richards and possibly others directed toward Simon, and now the trial is about to start."

Wow, this man wasn't popular, with a bunch of people, I thought to myself. I hadn't read anything about this. I had been occupied with the house and hadn't subscribed to the paper yet.

"He was on his way to meet with someone about a new story earlier in the evening yesterday," she said, more thinking out loud than speaking to me.

"Do you have any idea who he was meeting with or what it was about?" I asked, pulling her back to reality.

"No, I wish I did. Simon always kept his information very private. He wouldn't even divulge any details to Alan, our editor, until he had something concrete."

"So, when do you think you'll hear anything from the police?" I was trying not to quiz her too much.

"I'm supposed to head over to police headquarters in a couple of hours. We want to get at least a preliminary report before we go to press. You know I wanted to write more important stories, but not at Simon's expense. I would never do anything to hurt Simon; I could never hurt anyone, especially over a job."

I left, thinking Jillian seemed genuine. She didn't strike me as a killer. I did wonder why she felt the need to insist she had nothing to do with his murder. I couldn't help but wonder who Simon had the appointment with the night he died. Those questions swirled in my head.

CHAPTER ELEVEN

I CALLED Maggie after I got home and we agreed to meet that evening for dinner. We always had a good time together, but tonight we were a little subdued. There was a murder in our town and a murderer on the loose.

We sat in a high-sided booth toward the back of the restaurant.

"Look, brought you a copy," Maggie said, pulling a newspaper out of her bag.

"Have you read it?" I asked, taking the paper she offered.

"Yes, but I wasn't sure if you were getting the paper yet."

I read the brief story while we waited for our food. There were precious few details released by the police. Either they didn't know anything or they just weren't saying. Either way, the article left me with a lot of questions. I set the paper aside when our food arrived. We had ordered lasagna, salads and garlic bread. Carbs and more carbs with a salad on the side for good measure.

"So how are the tours going?" she asked while digging into her salad.

"Well, so far, I have only had two tours, but I have gotten some good information from the paper and the historical society. I've been able to expand my stories, and I am really enjoying myself."

"I'll have to pick a night and come out to join the tour," she laughed. "Except I don't want to go up to the old cemetery at night. I don't do cemeteries in the dark, they are way too creepy for me."

I laughed, "Nothing is going on up there, at least nothing I couldn't explain away. Although," I paused thinking back to what I had seen, "last night I thought that I saw something or someone in the woods behind the cemetery. Whoever or whatever it was disappeared down the hill." In my best spooky voice, I said, "So maybe something is going on up there." I heard a sharp coughing sound coming from the next booth, but Maggie's comments drew me back to our conversation.

"Stop it," Maggie peeped. "You're giving me the creeps."

We continued to enjoy our dinner and discussed cheerier topics for the rest of our meal.

"So, what do you think? Shall we splurge on dessert?" I asked.

"Of course, we should. Do you have to even ask that?" She laughed reaching for the small dessert menu.

We reviewed our options and finally settled on cannoli and coffee. "I am going to have to increase my activity and cut back on my carbs."

"Well, you could start your running again, just beware that you don't stumble across any dead bodies," Maggie teased me.

"Dead bodies are definitely not something I want to stumble across on a run," I said as I picked up the newspaper again.

We polished off our dessert, paid our check and stood to leave. I noticed Maggie stopped at the booth behind us. Priscilla sat in the booth by herself.

"Hey, Priscilla," she said. "I didn't see you sitting there, you could have joined us. Emily, this is Priscilla." Maggie proceeded to introduce us.

"Yes, I know," I said, extending my hand. I remembered what it was like to be the new person in town and wanted to be friendly. "I was over at Claudette's the other day when you came in. So, I guess you got the job with Maggie after all."

"Yes," Maggie continued, "and she's a whiz. She knows all about different plants, flowers, and I'm glad to have her."

"Well, I guess not getting that position at the newspaper was meant to be, otherwise you might not have ended up with Maggie. "

Priscilla gave an uneasy smile. "I guess you're right," she said.

"We'll leave you to finish up and next time say something and you can join us," Maggie admonished.

We stood outside and chatted for a few more minutes before we parted ways. I drove back home, thinking about what a nice evening I had after such a shocking morning. I thought back over the lack of information about the murder in the paper and how many people seemed to have had issues with Simon. I loved mysteries and puzzles, but this one involved a murder. I think a bit more poking about was called for.

CHAPTER TWELVE

THE NEXT MORNING dawned bright and clear. A good morning for a run, but I had to admit I was reluctant to take the trail by the river, which was my normal running path. And I was still mulling over the murder of Simon. I needed to find a way to speak with Dara, his widow, but how was I going to run into her without seeming too obvious? And then it hit me. A memory of my mother and her Southern charm. Take her a dish and pay your respects. I wasn't living in the South anymore, and I wondered if they did that here. It was as if my mother spoke to me saying, "*It's always good to be polite and show respect, no matter where you live.*" So, it was settled. I started cooking, again with a nod to Mom and days gone by, good ol' chicken and dumplings. Nothing says comfort, I thought, like a soothing bowl of chicken and dumplings.

While my meal was simmering, I settled down with my cup of coffee to review some more of the material I had received from Mrs. Smithers at the historical society. I loved reading history and this was a fascinating old town.

Copper Ridge was founded in the early 1800s as a

mining town. After a tunnel collapsed and claimed the lives of miners, the company decided to close the mine. The town had once been the county seat, but as bigger roads and interstates were built, Copper Ridge was bypassed and forgotten.

Fast forward to the present day, and the quaint almost-forgotten town now made most of its money from tourism. The Little Copper River runs down off the mountain and through the town. There was at least one company providing rafting tours. Local artisans had moved into the old previously abandoned downtown buildings, opening up art galleries, jewelry stores, quilt shops, gift shops, and candy stores. These businesses had revitalized the little town, breathing new life into the older restaurants and cafe.

I was brought out of my reverie by the smell of chicken and dumplings. With the tasty meal packed up and ready, I headed out. I drove up to Dara's house and parked at the curb. Her home was a Tudor style with an arched entry. Dara met me at the door. She was a lovely lady, just beginning to show a little age around her eyes, which might not have been as apparent except for the hint of dark circles there as well. She had light brown hair, styled in a perfect bob, impeccably dressed, complete with pearl earrings. "Hello, my name is Emily Rose and I hope I'm not intruding. I just wanted to come by and offer my condolences."

"Thank you, please come in," she graciously offered, stepping to one side. "Call me Dara."

"I am sorry to hear about Simon." I cringed inwardly. Well, I was sorry to hear about anyone's death or misfortune. I couldn't help it that I really didn't know Simon. "This is a recipe my mother used to make, and I know you might not feel like eating, but I wanted to bring you something."

"Thank you. That's so kind of you," she said as she took the container from me. "I'll just put this in the kitchen. Can I get you a cup of coffee or tea?"

"No, thank you, I don't want to put you to any trouble," I said.

"Please have a seat," she gestured toward the living room, "I'll put this in the kitchen and be right back."

I looked around; her home was spotless. Soft sage-colored walls in the living room, hardwood floors in the entryway, and a thick cream-colored carpet in the living room, which in fact looked like it had never been walked on. I took a seat on the equally cream-colored sofa as Dara re-entered the room.

"So how did you know Simon?" she asked.

"I met Simon at the paper. I had gone in to do research and met him there." I knew I was fudging this, because I never actually met him, heard him yes, and heard about him even more.

"Ah," she said, "well at least he hadn't written a story about you," she gave a slight smile. "If he had, you wouldn't have been so kind as to bring food." She tipped her chin up, "I'm a bit of a realist, Ms. Rose, I know what Simon could be like."

"Please, call me Emily." I looked over and saw the roses that Simon had sent to her the other day.

She followed my gaze, "Simon sent me those, the day before he died. I suppose he was trying to apologize, you see I suspected him of having an affair. I'm sorry, I don't mean to appear harsh, I guess I'm a bit tired. Tired of putting up with his moods, anxious about threats he received because of his stories." She sighed, "I suppose he had a lot going on."

"Threats?" I quizzed. I wondered how much she would be willing to divulge.

"Yes. That story he did about Mr. Richards didn't go over well with the town. As you probably know, Mr. Richards does a lot for this community, but Simon wrote a story about some possible illegal activities going on, some gambling and who knows what else. Simon started receiving threats after Mr. Richards was arrested. Sometimes phone calls, some notes left on his car, or on our doorstep. I thought they had stopped because it's been a while since we received anything." She murmured, "The police so far haven't figured out who it was."

"So how long have you and Simon called Copper Ridge home?" I asked, trying to lighten the subject a bit.

"I met Simon at college. He was born here, but his father moved the family away when he was younger. We moved back after Simon graduated from college." She said as she picked some invisible lint off her skirt.

"Do you and Simon get back home to visit his mother and father often?" It seemed like an innocent enough question, but I could see a shadow cross her eyes.

"Simon's mother passed away many years ago and he's not on speaking terms with his father. It seems his father had different career plans for Simon. They didn't see eye to eye, and neither one would give in. Simon loved journalism, had a passion for it. When he finished college, he moved away from home and never looked back. It's a shame; his father has been trying to get back in touch with him. He isn't well and wanted to make amends with his son, but as far as I know," she sighed "Simon hadn't returned any of his calls. Now I suppose it's too late. I only met the man once. I heard from other relatives that he remarried."

She sat silent for a second with a far-off look on her face. "What must you think of me?" she said, "prattling on about our problems."

"Not at all," I said sympathetically, reaching over to pat her hand. "Sometimes we all need someone to talk to. I've taken up enough of your morning," I said, then stood to leave. She walked me to the door. I turned and thanked her for her time. "If you ever need to talk again, I'm not too far away." I had told her where I live. As I got back in the car, I couldn't help but think she didn't strike me as a spouse bent on getting revenge. Maybe she was a good actress or maybe she was just remorseful after killing her husband.

CHAPTER THIRTEEN

I RETURNED HOME and had a voicemail waiting for me. Seems like Maggie had spoken with the police, and passed on my contact information. Detective Alex Mason had called and requested that I come down to the police station to make a statement. What do I know about Simon's murder? I didn't do it, I thought to myself, none too happy about the summons. Then it dawned on me. Duh, this would give me the perfect opportunity. I could speak with the detective about those calls and letters Simon had received. That thought made me look at my trip to see the detective in a whole new light.

I had a quick lunch, some leftover chicken and dumplings. Gosh, that was good, if I do say so myself. After eating, I left for the police department. It was one of the newer buildings in Copper Ridge located a couple of doors down from Maggie's Creations on the other end of the street from The Little Copper Cafe. It had a brick exterior with limestone trim and a wide double glass door entry. I entered the building, feeling my heartbeat quicken. Calm down I told myself, you're not in any trouble. I stopped at the front desk and asked for Detective Mason. He came out shortly to greet me. He was tall, over six feet, I suspected, although at five feet, three inches myself, everyone seemed tall. He had dark hair, dark eyes and a square jaw, which made him very rugged looking.

"Good afternoon, Ms. Rose, thank you for coming in," he said while extending his hand. "Come this way if you will." The desk sergeant buzzed us back through the door that Detective Mason had just come through. I followed him down the hallway to what appeared to be a small conference room. I sighed to myself. At least he didn't think of me as a suspect; otherwise, I'd likely be in an interrogation room.

"Glad to be of help," I said, "but I'm not sure what I have to offer."

Detective Mason motioned me to a seat on the side of the highly polished oval conference room table. He took a seat, dropping a tablet and file folder onto the table.

"Maggie tells me that you might have seen someone at the cemetery on the night that Simon was killed."

Bingo, I thought to myself, so this was a homicide. The other thing he had just revealed was Simon was killed at night.

"I had my ghost tour group up at the cemetery; it was the last stop on our tour. I had finished my story and was allowing time for my guests to wander around through the headstones a bit before coming back. I was waiting by the front gates facing toward the back of the cemetery when I thought I saw a shadow. When I looked again it appeared to be a person, but it was dark back there. If it was a person then they were dressed in dark-colored clothing. I'm sorry, I really don't know anything else."

"Do you think this would have been a male or a female?" the detective asked.

I hadn't even considered that it might be a woman, "Well, I suppose it could have been a woman. If it was a man, he wouldn't have been very tall. Whoever it was, they were stealthy. I mean it appeared they moved well in the limited light, quick and quiet."

"What direction were they moving?" he asked with a serious look on his face.

I stopped to consider his question. I knew the answer, but given my poor sense of direction, I wanted to be sure I phrased the answer correctly. He seemed to sense my hesitation.

"Hold on, I'll be right back," he said, rushing from the room. He returned with a map of the area including the cemetery, river, and path. I made note that there was a mark by the path and wondered if that's where the body was found. He pointed to the cemetery front gates and the cemetery boundary.

"The motion I saw was right here," I said, tracing the path of what I had seen. "But it moved very quickly, and then disappeared into the trees."

He asked a few more questions, including what time it was. I tried to be as helpful as possible, but I really didn't know anything else.

He started to roll up the map and I knew this was my moment. I pointed to the mark on the map, "So is that where Simon was found?"

"Did you know Simon?"

Without wanting to reveal too much about how little I actually knew him, I replied, "I know he was receiving threatening phone calls and notes." There was a look of surprise on his face. Great, I thought, now he's going to think I sent the notes.

I ventured on quickly, "So do you think his death had anything to do with the pending trial of Mr. Richards?"

"It's true he was getting threats in the form of calls and letters. So far, we have been unable to determine the origin," he admitted with a sigh.

I pressed my luck, "So how was he killed?"

He stood to walk me out. "I'm sorry, that's all I can say. Thank you for your time, I appreciate you coming in," he said, shaking my hand again. He spouted the usual law enforcement line, if I think of anything else, give him a call. Before you knew it I was back outside standing on the side-walk in the bright sunshine.

"Hey, how are you?" I turned and came face to face with Priscilla. "Did I see you coming out of the police station?"

"Hi there," I said, thinking it was always good to see a friendly face. "Yes, you did, but it was nothing, they were just asking me some questions."

I could tell that piqued her curiosity. "About Simon's murder?" she asked.

"Yes," I admitted, "but I really didn't know anything."

She didn't quite appear to be satisfied with my answer.

"Do you have time for a cup of coffee?" she asked.

"Can I get a rain check?" I needed to get back home to get ready for another tour. "How about dinner sometime this weekend with Maggie?"

"Of course," she agreed. "I'll look forward to it."

"Perfect, I'll touch base with Maggie and we will keep you updated." She waved goodbye as I turned to leave.

CHAPTER FOURTEEN

A FEW NIGHTS LATER, Maggie, Priscilla and I met up at the Three Pines Bistro & Tavern for a quiet dinner. The Three Pines had an open beam ceiling, hardwood floors, and exposed brick walls running the length of the building. The soft lighting made for a warm inviting atmosphere. There were booths and tables to one side and a bar on the other. We had plenty of options to choose from on their substantial menu. They served the standard soups, salads, and sandwiches as well as dinner entrees. I had finally settled on the broccoli and cheddar soup, with an order of their famous crusty cheesy bread. Their cheesy bread was one of my absolute favorites. The other two ladies ordered salads with grilled chicken.

We chatted easily as we began eating our food. I enjoyed my evening, thinking about how fortunate I was. I had a good home, in a charming little town, and the beginnings of new friendships.

"So how was Simon's funeral?" I asked Maggie. I hadn't attended. I might have led Detective Mason and Dara to believe I knew Simon more than I actually did, but I wasn't sure about attending his funeral.

"Dara was very brave. I know she had seen an attorney about a divorce, but still, they had been together for so long. There were still feelings there," Maggie said, shaking her head. "She is such a lovely lady. You know, Simon seemed to have everything a person could want, and yet over the years, he had grown more and more difficult to deal with. He definitely made enemies with the types of stories he wrote."

"I wonder if there was an underlying problem," Priscilla asked.

I didn't know how much information I wanted to pass on. "Well, Dara did share with me that he had a falling out with his father. That just goes to show you how little we actually know about others." I left it at that, not feeling comfortable with what I had said already.

"Detective Mason was at the funeral too. Suppose he was checking to see who would show up," Maggie said.

A little while later our waitress came by to check on us. I couldn't help but notice she waited until Priscilla was away from the table. "You know your friend was in here the other night with that guy who was murdered."

Maggie and I looked at each other in disbelief. "I didn't know she knew Simon," I said, looking at Maggie.

"When she came into my shop, she told me she had a pending job at the paper that had fallen through." Maggie was staring at me, neither of us knowing exactly what to think.

"I suppose since Simon worked at the paper, maybe they did know each other. Maybe he had promised her a position there. Funny she didn't mention that to us, though, as much as we have been talking about him." The waitress shrugged her shoulders and wandered off. "Don't say anything to Priscilla," I whispered. We didn't have time for further discussion as Priscilla walked back up to our table.

We were finishing up our coffee and Maggie started in. "You should have seen some of the arrangements Priscilla helped me with for Simon's funeral, they were so pretty. I'm grateful for the extra help you've given me. I suppose that was the newspaper's loss. So, did Simon promise you a job over there?" My eyes got big and I resisted the urge to nudge Maggie under the table, but Priscilla didn't seem to notice.

"No, it was Alan, the owner, who I had talked to over there about a possible job. I never met Simon." She said it so smoothly, but was that a twitch of nervousness I saw in her eyes? Could the waitress be mistaken? It was possible.

Maggie kept on going, "Well, Alan never knew a good thing when he saw it."

I had sat in stunned silence this whole time, not knowing what to say. Maggie looked at me, grinning with a sparkle in her eyes.

We finished up there, paid our checks and walked outside. I loved the night in Copper Ridge. Living in the city had never offered many opportunities for stargazing. I was troubled by what the waitress said about Priscilla. I couldn't help but wonder what Alan would say if I asked him about Priscilla's would-be job. But I didn't exactly know how to bring that up in conversation. I mulled it over in my head. Then I remembered, Jillian had said Simon was going to meet someone about a new story. Was Priscilla a source for his new story? If so, I couldn't help but wonder what it was about.

Maggie and Priscilla had said their goodbyes and were looking at me. I hadn't been paying any attention and had no idea what they had said. Maggie tried to cover for me.

"Emily, are you thinking up a new ghost story?"

I laughed, trying hard not to make it sound forced. "Hey, you know I don't make those stories up." I said my goodbyes to both of the ladies and headed home, thoughts swirling around in my head.

I lay in bed that night, unable to fall asleep. I finally got up, padding to the kitchen to make myself a cup of cocoa. I climbed back in bed, pulling my down comforter up and sipping my cocoa. My mind began to review my list of suspects, which was getting longer all the time.

Mr. Richards was still out on bond, pending the start of his trial. Illegal gambling or illegal business deals were a far cry from murder, but his life would never be the same again. Even if he was cleared of all charges, he might still be looked at suspiciously. He had a profitable business in Copper Ridge but Simon had made sure his reputation was ruined. Men have killed for less.

Jillian, the up and coming reporter, had high expectations for herself. I knew they argued with each other over news coverage. Simon had been very condescending, and her career would not have gone anywhere with Simon around. I would bet she was going to be getting a promotion soon; after all, she was the reporter covering this murder case.

Maybe Dara, the scorned spouse, got tired of putting up with him. Maybe she had enough and didn't want to wait for a divorce. No splitting the assets, just get rid of him and keep all the property.

And then there was Priscilla. I had no idea how she fit in. I didn't know anything about her, except she was good with plants, making flower arrangements, and she supposedly lied about knowing Simon.

What I didn't know yet was how Simon was killed.

Maybe a trip back to see Detective Mason was called for. After all, I could share with him the news about Priscilla being with Simon the night he died. I wondered if he already knew that.

I finished my cocoa, fluffed up my feather pillow and decided to give falling asleep another try. Next thing I knew the sun was shining through my bedroom window.

CHAPTER FIFTEEN

I KNEW I could call Detective Mason, but a trip to his office might be a bit more fruitful. I wanted to tell Maggie that I was going in to see him, but I didn't want to run into Priscilla. I went over to the coffee shop and picked up two lattes, wondering to myself if Detective Mason was a coffee drinker. Ha, of course he was, I thought to myself, he's a police officer. Oh, that was way too stereotypical of me. Behave, I told myself.

I entered police headquarters with my two lattes and asked to see Detective Mason. Another detective was walking by and offered to take me back. He showed me to the detective's desk, offered me a chair and said he'd go get Detective Mason for me. I set the lattes down on his desk. I knew this was my chance. With no one else around I took a quick look at the top of his desk and opened the folder with Simon's name on it. Jackpot! The coroner's report was on top and it listed a head wound, so it looked like someone had hit him over the head.

Then I spotted the toxicology report, some alcohol in his blood, not much.

I heard approaching footsteps, so I hurriedly closed the folder and took a seat in the chair, picked up a coffee and tried my best to look innocent.

Detective Mason walked up. "Good morning," I said, holding out a coffee cup to him. "I hope you like lattes." His eyes lit up, although I was uncertain if it was because of the coffee or because he was happy to see me. Oh my, I thought to myself, where did that thought come from? Of course, he was happy to get the latte.

"Ms. Rose," he said, smiling and taking the coffee I offered. "Thank you. So, what brings you in today? Did you think of any new information for me?"

"Well, yes, I suppose I did. I was having dinner over at the Three Pines last evening. A waitress there said Simon was in there the night he died and was with Priscilla Barnes."

He pulled out his notebook and wrote down her name. "Do you happen to have a phone number for Ms. Barnes?" he asked.

"No, but she is working with Maggie in her shop."

"Maggie the florist?"

"Yes, that's the one."

"We tracked Simon's credit card to the Three Pines. We knew it was used there before his death. So far, we hadn't found any employees who confirmed seeing him there that night. Maybe that waitress was off the day I stopped by. Anyway, I'm scheduled to go back over there again."

I passed on the name of the waitress. "I'll go over there today and speak with her."

I watched as he wrote down her name in his notebook and picked up my coffee. If he noticed the folder on his desk a little askew, he didn't say anything.

"Thank you for coming in and for the coffee." He said, lifting his cup to take a sip. "Here, let me walk you out."

I stood on the sidewalk outside of police headquarters sipping my coffee and thinking. So, Simon had a head injury, someone hit him over the head. It doesn't sound like something a lady could do. Was it possible that Mr. Richards caught up with him or had he hired someone to take his revenge?

CHAPTER SIXTEEN

I WAS EXCITED. I had another tour tonight and I planned on including another stop. I met my group at the hotel. Two couples had come to town for a long weekend of hiking and rafting.

"Hello," I said as they approached.

"Hi," they replied. "We're here for the tour," one of the men said. "I'm Mike and this is Pat, Kim, and Wally."

"Then you're in the right place. My name is Emily and I'll be your tour guide tonight."

Pat spoke up, "We heard about your tour from Claudette and thought it would be fun."

I smiled, "Ah, so you've been to The Little Copper Cafe."

"Yes," Wally laughed patting his belly, "and the food was amazing."

"I agree with you. It's one of my favorite places to eat," I said. "It's just us tonight, so let's get started, shall we?"

We made the usual stops at the hotel, courthouse, old stone jail, and Evergreen Manor. Then we made our way over to the Carriage House.

"This is the Carriage House," I said with a sweep of my arm. "As you can see, it's a lovely three-story Victorian. The home was originally owned by the town banker. He and his family had moved to town and had the house custom-built. They had always enjoyed the finer things, so many of the furnishings were shipped in from back East. The beautiful stained-glass window was made and shipped over from Italy and has remarkably survived all these years. The family, it seems, loved to host elaborate parties.

Kim spoke up, "That house is gorgeous. I've always loved Victorians with their wrap-around porches."

"It's a miracle that stained-glass window has remained intact." Pat looked at me, "So has the house remained in the same family?"

"No, unfortunately, years after the family died, the home was sold. Since then it's been used for many different things, including a brothel, a boarding house, a temporary stopover for small troop movements, and even an office building. It had fallen into disrepair but was recently purchased and restored. Now it's a bed and breakfast, full of old charm and lots of antiques, from what I hear. Guests that have stayed there have reported hearing things. As the stories go, they hear things that sound like a party, such as people talking and laughing, music and the sounds of glasses clinking together. It seems the banker and his family are pleased with the restoration and they are again hosting their parties there."

"Well, at least the spirits hanging around in there sound happy," Kim laughed.

"Yes, I agree." I walked my guests back through town and passed several shops on the way back to the Gage Hotel.

"I just love this town," Pat said as she stopped to look in

one of the shop windows. She turned to look at Kim, "I think we should do some shopping tomorrow before we go."

Wally laughed, "As long as I get to go back to the cafe for pancakes, then I don't mind what you ladies do."

"I'm with you Wally, the pancakes at the cafe are the best I've ever had. Enjoy them." About that time, we walked up in front of the hotel. "Here we are folks," I said handing out the drink tickets. "I hope you have enjoyed the tour. And watch out, you never know, you might see the ghost of Mr. Gage tonight," I said to them laughingly.

CHAPTER SEVENTEEN

LYING in bed the next morning, I was thinking again about Simon's murder, which really seemed to occupy my mind. Being hit over the head sounded like something a man would do, at least that was my personal opinion. I needed to switch the focus and look at James Richards. Or maybe he hired someone to take care of Simon. I knew very little about Mr. Richards and wasn't sure if I even wanted to approach him myself.

I could read the stories about his arrest and upcoming trial in the paper, but nothing would be as good as a personal interview. I wondered to myself if I could pretend to be someone and make it into his home to speak with him. He was out on bond, pending the start of his trial. I continued to contemplate my dilemma as I drank my coffee and I finally figured it out. I was going to pretend that I was a junior legal aide, going over his story. It would get me inside and then I could hopefully have a conversation with him.

I searched online and read a bunch of the recent stories that had been written about Mr. Richards. It seems like he had been a former financial planner and investment coordinator. He was accused of taking money that he was supposed to be investing and gambling with it. He had a history of being generous to the town, but I wondered if he was being generous with other people's money. From the stories I read, his gambling had very recently gotten out of control, and people were starting to suspect that things weren't quite right. Jillian and Simon had caught wind of this and the rest is history. The newspaper reports made everything seem very cut and dry. On the other hand, Mr. Richards seemed to have a loyal following in town. His supporters couldn't believe that he could be part of anything so dishonest.

I went over to his home, a modest ranch-style home on a quiet tree-lined street. Mr. Richards answered the door when I rang the bell. He looked a little scruffy and in need of a shave.

"Mr. Richards," I began. "I am a junior legal aide, and I'm hoping you'll let me go over your case." He had a bewildered look on his face, so I talked quickly. "Your case is still being handled by your legal team, I'm just trying to get some interviewing practice. Would you be willing to speak with me?" I asked with the best innocent look I could manage.

He rubbed his stubbled chin and nodded. "I'd love some company, I'm not getting out much these days."

He opened his door and showed me in. His home was a little musty smelling, like a house that had been closed up too long. His living room was off to the left and a dining room off to the right. Both were dark with the heavy drapes pulled over the windows. He kept on walking and I followed him, down a dark hallway ending up in a surprisingly sunny kitchen at the back of his house. He motioned me to a seat at the table. I looked around, checking to see where the back door was. After all, Simon was possibly murdered by this man and I was now alone with him in his home.

I pulled out a legal tablet, trying to look like I knew what I was doing. "I have read the charges against you, but if you will please, tell me your side of the story."

"I have been a businessman in this town for over twenty years and I am innocent of all these charges. I realize everyone says they're innocent, but I am. I know it looks bad, but I had a young intern working with me this summer. He was the one who took my clients' money. He was the one who ran the gambling ring."

He went on to tell me his story in detail and I made notes. After he paused and appeared to have finished, I felt safe enough to ask a few questions, trying to make it sound chatty.

"So, I suppose you have plenty of time to read the papers. Have you heard that the reporter who broke your story is now dead? It appears that someone might have hit him over the head."

"Yes, I heard he died," he said, shaking his head. "But I didn't know how and I certainly didn't have anything to do with that. I would never kill anyone."

"Do you get out of the house much?"

"No, not at all. Like I said before, I'm a spectacle now anytime I leave the house." He sat frowning at me.

"Your house isn't too far away from the river trail where Simon was found. That's not going to look good for you."

He stiffened and his tone grew harsh. "Look here, missy, what are you trying to say? Just because he made my life a nightmare and because I live close to where his body was found that I must have had something to do with his murder? Do you see this?" He turned and I was about to bolt for the back door, when he raised his right arm barely to shoulder height. "That's as high as my right arm can go, I have a shoulder injury and if like you said, he was hit over the head, I couldn't get my arm up high enough to give him a good whack. My arm is so weak I have problems even combing my hair. And yes, I'm right-handed."

He shook his head and wandered off to make himself something to drink. "I'm sorry," he said, "it seems like when people think you are guilty of one crime, then you're guilty of something else."

I gathered my things. "I'm sorry, Mr. Richards, I didn't mean to upset you." I left, letting myself out the front door. I didn't mean to upset him, but if he were telling me the truth, it would have been difficult for him to have committed this murder. Now I was hoping he wouldn't mention my visit to his lawyer. As I approached my car, which I had parked on the other side of the street, I couldn't help but feel like I was being watched. I took a brief glance around but didn't notice anyone. I could only suppose that it was Mr. Richards watching me retreat to the safety of my car. I hurried on my way, feeling I was no closer to solving this crime than I was the day I started.

CHAPTER EIGHTEEN

I WENT HOME and changed my clothes; it was time for a run. I had put it off for long enough. The running trail by the river had been one of my favorite places to run. I had some doubts today about running that particular trail; after all, this was where Simon's body was found. Come on, I told myself, it's broad daylight. What could possibly go wrong? I tied my shoes and stood up straight, thinking life is too short to be ruled by fear, and out the door I went.

The first mile was always the hardest, but I kept on going. I began to get a rhythm going now, as I cut through a nearby parking lot. The day was bright and sunny, a vivid blue sky with no clouds to be seen. I turned onto the trail which brought me down by the river, the sounds of the water tumbling over the rocks were so soothing. I imagined there would be wildflowers growing along this trail in the springtime and I was definitely going to have to try out the rafting next summer. I ran while I listened to the wind blowing through the nearby trees and loved how it sounded. The dirt path changed to concrete and there were benches scattered along the trail facing the water. I couldn't help but think that the concrete path made it easy for anyone to access this part of the river, including where Simon was found.

I continued down the concrete path for another couple of miles, then I turned around to head back home. I loved running. It always helped me think.

As I approached the trailhead, I looked across the parking lot and saw Detective Mason. He waved at me as I approached. "I see that having a killer on the loose isn't keeping you inside."

"Well, it was such a pretty day, and I needed to clear my head and do some thinking," I admitted.

"Thinking about what?" he queried.

I suppose that came with being a police officer. I hung my head for a moment, standing there with my hands on my hips. I raised my head and looked him squarely in the eyes. "I have heard things about Simon, threats that were made, and honestly I was trying to figure out who had killed him. I know, it's none of my business, but I can't help it."

"Well, you need to try to help it," he said a bit sternly. "You wouldn't want to find yourself in a sticky situation."

"I know, and I don't mean to interfere in any way. And I promise if I see anyone coming at me with a baseball bat, I'll run the other direction. As you can see, I'm a pretty good runner."

"Baseball bat?" he asked, wrinkling his brow.

"Yes, I heard Simon was hit on the head or at least that's what I heard," I admitted, wondering if he would spill any information.

Detective Mason sighed, "Simon might have had a head injury, but that's not what killed him."

"Well, if the head injury didn't kill him, what did?"

"You know, I'm not at liberty to say anything else about

an ongoing investigation. Keep your eyes open, try to resist the urge to poke your nose into other people's business and leave the police work to the police."

If I had heard that from some other person, I might have been irritated, but when he said it, well, it sounded sincere like he was concerned.

"Well, I'll see if I can keep my nose where it belongs," I laughed, tapped the end of my nose, and turned to continue my run.

CHAPTER NINETEEN

I BOUNDED up onto the porch following my run, feeling accomplished. That's when I caught sight of a white piece of paper. It was partially tucked under my front doormat. I pulled it out and unlocked my door. I dropped the note and door key onto my table and walked into the kitchen to get a drink of water. I picked up the phone while I was still sipping my water and gave Maggie a call. I had no tours that night and I thought it would be a good night for dinner if she was free. I got her voicemail. Thinking she must be busy with a customer, I left her a brief voicemail asking her to call me back when she had a moment. I glanced over and remembered the note. I'm not sure what I thought would be on the piece of paper, but I sure didn't expect what I was looking at.

It read, 'I know what you're doing. Stop looking into Simon's murder now, if you know what's good for you.'

I sat down hard in a dining room chair. I was still holding the note, but my hands were shaking. I hopped up from my chair and peered out my front windows, but saw nothing out of the ordinary. I flung open the front door and ran down my walk, looking up and down my empty quiet street, feeling anxious and angry all at the same time. There didn't appear to be anyone around that didn't belong. I turned to walk back into the house, glancing over my shoulder, because how could a note like that not spook me? I heard the phone ring and I hurried in to grab it.

"Hello," I said, anxious to get ahold of Maggie. I listened, but there was no one there. "Hello," I said a little louder. Still nothing. Next a dial tone blared in my ear. I looked at my phone, although I'm not sure what I expected to see. I clicked the button and put the phone down, still keeping my eyes on it. After a moment, I thought to myself, this is ridiculous.

I turned to walk away when the phone rang again. I couldn't help but jump slightly when it rang. I jerked up the phone. "Hello," I said rather sharply.

"Hey there." Maggie paused, "What's up?"

"Did you just call me?" I asked her.

"Nope, not me. I just listened to your voicemail. Are you okay?" she asked with a hint of concern in her voice.

I thought to myself, it takes a real friend to know there is something wrong when so little was said. "I'm okay. I had actually called to see if you wanted to come over for dinner tonight."

"Sure, I'd love to," Maggie answered. "Are you sure you're okay? No offense, but you sound a little off."

"Well don't freak or anything, seems like someone left me a note on my doorstep, basically warning me off. Seems like I must have gotten too close to someone while looking into Simon's murder."

"What?! Hang up, you need to call the police." Maggie practically screeched into the phone.

"I'm not sure what they can do. I've been holding the

note, and not sure they could get fingerprints off of it. And it's typed. But it's obvious I've upset someone," I admitted.

"Are you sure you're okay? Do you need me to come over?" Maggie volunteered.

"No, I'm okay. I think it was just someone trying to scare me."

She gave a sharp laugh, "Well they have succeeded in scaring me and I wasn't the one who got the note. Please be careful. And keep your phone close and check your doors. Are they all locked?"

I looked around the living room warily, "They're locked, but I promise I'll go recheck them when we hang up." Now it was me who was trying to calm her down. "Ok, so see you tonight?"

"Yes, sure, I'll be there. Call if you have any issues; no, scratch that, call the police," Maggie said firmly.

I gave a little laugh. "Don't worry. It'll be fine. See you tonight." I tried to sound calm, and hoped this would put her at ease.

CHAPTER TWENTY

LATER THAT DAY, after standing in front of the pantry and freezer for a while, I finally decided on fettuccine Alfredo with chicken, a nice salad, and crispy garlic bread. I laughed, thinking bread was always a winner. I had the chicken and sauce finished, the bread in the oven, and I was finishing up the salad and pasta when Maggie knocked at the door.

I opened up the door and Maggie stood with a lovely Christmas cactus. It was beautiful.

"Hey, you're just in time, come on in," I said, stepping aside to let her in.

She held out the plant to me and said, "For you, a housewarming gift, a little late, but at least it's budding now."

"Thank you, I love it and I have just the place for it." I placed it on one of my end tables, admiring the tiny pink buds spilling over the edges of the pot. I think it should get the right amount of light here. "That's so sweet of you. But wait, I thought these plants only bloom around Christmas or so?"

"I did a forced bloom. It's easy. I just put it in a cool and dark place and that will force it to bloom. By the way, these are also known as a Thanksgiving cactus or a holiday cactus." Maggie was in complete florist mode now. "But whatever it's called, I hope you enjoy it."

"I will, thanks again. Are you hungry? It's almost ready!"

"I'm starving, we were slammed today and I didn't have time for lunch. But I'd rather be busy than sitting there waiting for the phone to ring. And are you okay? I was really worried about you."

"Perfectly fine. Go ahead and pull up a chair and I'll put things on the table."

"Here, I'll help you," Maggie offered and in just a minute we were seated and enjoying our dinner.

"There is nothing like buttery, crispy-crusted garlic bread," Maggie said serving herself another piece of bread.

"I know," I said with my eyes closed, relishing every bite.

We chatted about various things, and then moved on to more serious topics.

"So, where's the note?" Maggie asked me, wiping her hands on her napkin.

I got up and brought back a large clear zippered storage bag. "I don't know if it will do any good to have it in the bag. If I do turn it in to the police, maybe they can dust it for prints. I don't know if it will have any fingerprints on it," I sighed, "other than mine."

Maggie took the bag from me, looking at me seriously. "What do you mean if you turn it in to the police? Why wouldn't you turn this in?" She continued to scan the note.

"Well I don't know, it's probably nothing." I shrugged,

taking the bag back from her. "I mean, what can they do about it, besides tell me to mind my own business?"

"It doesn't sound like nothing. This is serious and you need to take it seriously," Maggie warned me.

I remembered my other news. "Guess what I heard today?" Not waiting for a response, I launched in on my story. "I was out for a run today and I ran into Detective Mason, who told me Simon didn't die from a blow to the head. He wouldn't tell me how he died though."

She had a puzzled look on her face, "What made you think he died from a blow to the head?"

I paused, mostly because I knew she wasn't going to like what I had to say. "Well, I went to see Detective Mason one day. I was sitting by his desk waiting for him," I paused again, "and I sort of took a peek at a folder on his desk It had Simon's name on it."

"You did what?" Her voice rising. "Are you out of your mind?"

"Well, no one was in the room and the file was sitting right there. Unfortunately, I didn't have much time. I only got a glance before I had to close the folder up. No one saw me," I said, trying to justify my actions.

She sat there with her mouth open and a shocked look on her face. "I can't believe you. You shouldn't be doing things like that," she paused, "but since you did, it's too bad you didn't get a better look."

I grinned at her, shrugging my shoulders, holding my hands up in surrender until we both laughed.

"But all this time," I sighed, "I thought if he was hit over the head, then the killer could have been Mr. Richards or even someone he hired. If he died from something else, then it could have been anyone and I'm right back to square one. There has got to be a way to get more information. I just haven't figured out how to do it. It's not like I can break into the police department overnight and rummage through their files."

"Well, at least you know where to draw the line," Maggie said, taking a bite of garlic bread. "I'd hate for you to get caught, then I'd have to bail you out of jail. Earth to Emily," Maggie laughed, noticing my far-off look.

"I'm sorry, I'm just stumped and not sure how I'm going to figure this out," I moaned.

"Well, since when is solving this crime your job?" she asked. "Are you picking up a second job with the police?"

"No, of course not," I whined, "but aren't you curious?"

"Not curious enough, I suppose. I'm happy just letting the police do their job. It's safer that way. If you left it to the police, then maybe you wouldn't get threatening notes on your doorstep either." She gave me a pointed look as she got up to take her plate to the kitchen.

"I know, you're probably right," I relented, "but it's almost like I can't help it. I see a puzzle and I want to solve it."

"A puzzle is one thing, but murder is something completely different. Ooh," she said when she saw me uncover a plate of brownies. "I love brownies like you love solving puzzles." We sat down to enjoy our dessert. I knew she was right. I should just leave it alone.

CHAPTER TWENTY-ONE

TWO MORE NIGHTS of successful tours and I was starting to feel more comfortable with them. I knew as the weather turned colder, my crowds would be getting smaller and smaller, but spring and summer should make up for that. Things had calmed down and I had no further notes or phone calls.

"So, what did you think?" I asked Claudette. She had shown up for my tour tonight and it was a nice surprise.

"I loved it! You know I've lived here my whole life and I didn't know those stories you told. I was thoroughly entertained. Listen, if you have a moment, I have some news for you."

"Sure, how about a cup of coffee? Let's go into the hotel," I suggested. We ordered our coffee and took a small table in the corner of the bar. It was quiet in there tonight.

"So, what's up?" I asked.

"Do you remember when Priscilla came into the cafe the morning we first met her? Didn't she say she had spoken with Alan about a job at the paper?"

I thought back, "Ah, yes, she did." Seemed like an innocent enough comment.

"Well, Alan happened in the other day. You know, he and I go way back. We were in school together. We didn't hang out then, he was a couple of years ahead of me." She was rambling, but I sat quietly, knowing she'd get to the point.

"Anyway, he came in and when it got quiet we started chatting. I made some offhand comment about him losing a good worker in Priscilla and that she seems to be doing a good job over for Maggie at her shop. He had no idea what I was talking about. He said he didn't know anyone named Priscilla. I pressed him a little more, and finally specifically asked if he had offered her a job. He was adamant. He finally looked at me and asked if there was anything wrong with my hearing. He said he didn't offer her a job, he never met her, and was not even familiar with anyone by that name. About that time, a couple walked through the door and I didn't get another chance to talk to him. Even if I had, I'm not sure what difference it would have made. He was very adamant, he'd never heard of her."

My mouth must have been hanging open because after a moment she said, "Close your mouth, dear." I dropped my head and grinned; that is exactly something my mother would have said. Still, I was trying to process what she had told me.

"So, what do you think?" she asked.

I had been sitting there mulling over this new information. "I don't know. Why would Priscilla say something like that?" Now I had another puzzle to solve.

"What do we do next?" Claudette's eyes were sparkling, and she was ready to attack this discrepancy.

I sure didn't want to put her in any danger though. I

tried to play things down. "Maybe it was a slip of the tongue, maybe she meant to say Simon. I heard they met for drinks over at the Three Pines." Oops, shouldn't have said that. That comment made her all the more eager to figure out what was going on with Priscilla.

Claudette took a sip of her coffee, obviously not satisfied with my explanation.

I tried again. "We don't do anything. Who knows, maybe she has her reasons for wanting her privacy."

She still didn't like my explanation, but was content to leave it alone. We drank our coffee and moved onto less puzzling topics of conversation.

CHAPTER TWENTY-TWO

I POPPED into Maggie's shop the next day. "Are we alone?" I mouthed the question, glancing around the front room as I entered.

"Yep, it's just us. What's up?" Maggie asked.

I relayed the information I had picked up from Claudette the night before. Maggie was as puzzled as I was.

"Do you happen to have a copy of her employment application or resume?"

"Well, no. I hired her sort of on the recommendation of Alan," she admitted, shaking her head. "Oh my, I should have known better, but she's an awesome worker. I have had absolutely no issues with her." She thought for a minute, "How about I do this, I'll get her to fill out a job application and ask for a resume. I can tell her I need it to make sure my files are in order. It's a bit questionable, but maybe she won't even think about it, especially if I try to be low key about it."

"Ok, sounds like a good plan. Give it a shot and let me know what happens. If you manage to get a resume you can let me see it." I planned to delve into her background and see what I could find. For now, I'd have to wait to see what would happen.

I stopped by the store on my way home to pick up a few things. As I pulled into the small parking lot, I couldn't help but notice Dara standing by her car talking to someone. I didn't recognize the woman she was speaking to. I parked my car, turned it off and slumped down in my seat. Yes, I was going to eavesdrop.

Dara was agitated and was speaking rather loudly; I guess that's what had caught my attention in the first place. That could also be why she didn't even notice my arrival a couple of spots away. "I don't know how I ever put up with that man. There were times when I wanted to hit him upside the head. You know he had a falling out with his father. His father had been trying to get in touch with him over the last year. Simon was so stubborn, he wouldn't return any of his calls, he wanted nothing to do with him. It used to make me so angry. Not that I care about the money, but Simon's family is loaded. Simon was one of those born with a silver spoon in his mouth and he could have cared less about his family or their money. Newspaper reporters don't exactly make a prime salary." Dara paused in her rant, "Oh, what must I sound like? I'm not money hungry, but would a little extra money have hurt?"

The other lady had been standing there listening and nodding her head. She was speaking more quietly than Dara and trying to be comforting, "I know this has to be incredibly rough, I couldn't imagine what you must be going through, losing Simon."

"Well, at least your husband is supportive and appears to be very caring. Simon could be so arrogant and hard-headed. I don't know what I ever saw in him."

Dara hung her head, "Oh, I don't know what I'm saying.

Stages of grief, I suppose. I was angry at him when he was alive and now, I'm angry that he's gone and left me." Her friend hugged her and they said their goodbyes.

Well, Dara had quite the temper. Who knew a temper like that could be wrapped up in that woman? Was she actually a little money hungry? It sounds like she really could have done him in after all.

CHAPTER TWENTY-THREE

AFTER I LEFT THE STORE, I headed back home, continuing to mull over the conversation I had overheard between Dara and her friend. I was trying to put all the random pieces of the puzzle together, but not being very successful.

As I turned in my driveway, I happened to look to the right, noticing a strange car parked just down the road a bit. The sun was glinting off the windshield so I couldn't see if the car was occupied or not. My little dead-end street was very short and typically very quiet. Over the past several months I had noticed a pattern of the neighbors' comings and goings. Most of the neighbors worked during the day, but who knows, maybe someone had company.

I didn't give it further thought, lugging in my groceries. I happened to glance at the dining room table, spotting the note still in the plastic bag. It was sitting in the same spot where Maggie and I had dinner. I hadn't taken it to the police station as of yet. In thinking it over, I realized Maggie was probably right. Maybe I should take it in and at least make a report.

I finished putting away my things and snagged the clear bag off the table. I hopped back in the car and headed back to town. I stopped at the intersection and looked back, happening to see the car pull away from the curb. The sun was still shining on the windshield, making it impossible to even tell if it was a lady or man behind the wheel. The car followed me into town, but then again, living in a small town with limited exits, this wouldn't be a big coincidence. Maybe I was just being paranoid, but the hairs on the back of my neck were telling me different.

I circled the town square, and returned to park in front of the police station. I sat in my car looking around, but the strange vehicle was no longer in sight. I told myself I must be imagining things. I looked up to see Detective Mason watching me from the sidewalk. I climbed out of the car, trying not to look spooked.

"Are you okay?"

He was obviously very observant. I knew I needed to explain, but I also didn't want to come off sounding like a paranoid needy ditz either. I sighed and started in. "Yes, I'm fine, but maybe if you have a moment we can talk."

"Sure. Do you need to come into the office?"

"Yes, I think I do."

He got a serious look on his face, "Then let's go."

He walked me into the police station down the drab colorless hallway. I couldn't help but wonder why police stations had to look so dreary. Would it kill them to have a little color in the place? He offered me a chair by his desk.

"So, you seemed a little spooked when you drove up. You want to tell me what's going on?"

"This," I said, reaching into my tote and pulling out the plastic bag with the note. I handed it over to him.

He looked it over, seeming to read it multiple times.

"Where did you get this? Was there an envelope?"

"That day you saw me out on the run, it was waiting for me under my doormat when I got back home."

"That was days ago. Why didn't you bring it in sooner?"

"Maggie told me to bring it in, but I didn't think it was important. I figured it was just some crackpot.

"That doesn't explain the look on your face today when you drove up." He was in full detective mode now.

"It was probably nothing, but there was a car that I didn't recognize in the neighborhood today. I had been out shopping and I noticed it when I got back home. It sort of followed me when I left to come here, but really," I said, shaking my head, "that could have just been a coincidence."

"What did it look like?"

I gave him a description of the car as best I could. I knew what was coming next and mentally I was kicking myself because I didn't have a good answer.

"How about a plate number?"

There it was. "No, it was too far away," but the truth is I was too rattled to notice much. I should have paid more attention. I could feel my emotions switching from fear and apprehension to outright anger. How dare someone follow me? "I should have circled the square and tried to follow them."

"No, you shouldn't. Don't be going off by yourself doing anything crazy. You hear me?" He was giving me a look that meant business. "Now back to this note. I'm not sure how much we can get from it. No envelope, a typed note with nothing special about the paper, but we'll check it for prints. Now here's my other question for you. What have you done that would make someone feel the need to write a note like this?"

Now he'd done it. "Me? I didn't do anything." Wow, was that defensive or what? I thought to myself.

"You obviously did something. I'm not saying you're the bad guy here, because you're not. It could have even been something inadvertently said or done that has ticked this person off." He looked at me with a sparkle in his eyes, "So have you been out there interviewing suspects, by any chance?"

My hands were getting clammy, "No, of course not." I told him a bald-faced lie, although I was fairly certain he could see right through me.

"Listen, be careful. We don't know who killed Simon. We have several suspects and are following up on some leads, but it's taking time. Please, be careful what you say and to whom you say it. And if you see any cars that don't seem to belong in your neighborhood, then give us a call. We'll come over and check it out, okay?"

"Okay, I get it. And thanks, I'll be careful." He walked me back out and I caught him taking a look around the square for any car matching the description I'd given him. But there was nothing out of the ordinary for him to see. I left the station feeling like at least he had taken my concerns seriously.

CHAPTER TWENTY-FOUR

"HEY!" Maggie called as Priscilla entered the shop. "Thanks for dropping off that last order for me."

"Sure, no problem, glad to help," Priscilla said as she made her way to the back to hang up her jacket. "It's windy out there today," she said smoothing her hair back in place.

"Yes, it sure it. Just wait until winter sets in, did you get a lot of snow from where you were from?" Maggie was fishing for information.

"No, not too much."

"Listen, I need to get some of my paperwork in order. My business manager is requesting paperwork for all my employees. So, if you will fill out this application, attach your resume to it and get it back to me," Maggie said, handing Priscilla the employee application.

Priscilla took the forms, "Ok, sure, no problem." She tried to sound convincing, but Maggie thought she saw a bit of reluctance in her eyes.

Maggie watched her walk off, hoping her story was plausible enough. She didn't want to raise any suspicions.

She had no business manager, but Priscilla didn't need to know that and we need that information, or more accurately put, Emily needed it.

CHAPTER TWENTY-FIVE

LATER THAT NIGHT my phone rang and I was a little surprised as I answered; it was Mr. Richards.

"I'm sorry to intrude on your evening, but I wanted to apologize if I was a bit harsh at the end of our meeting. That's not the kind of man I am. I just wanted you to know that."

"I understand how rough all this must be for you."

"Do you? Have you ever been accused of a crime before?" his voice rising. "Has anyone ever called your character into question?" There was a pause on the other end of the phone and I heard him sigh, "There I go again, running off at the mouth. This whole situation has been quite stressful and even after the trial, I'm not sure if my life will ever be normal again."

"You're right, Mr. Richards, I don't know what it's like. It has to be really frustrating for people to presume that you are guilty before your day in court. I'm sure it's even worse to think about being linked to Simon's murder."

"It is unfathomable. I've always tried to do the right thing for the people of this town and now this. Again, I'm sorry if I sounded rude. Please accept my apologies. You have a good evening and stay safe," he admonished.

With that, he hung up and I was left listening to a dial tone. I hung up the phone. It was an odd phone call, and I wasn't sure how he managed to get my home phone number. My business number was listed, but my home number was not and the thought that he found it was making me a bit uncomfortable. I know I never mentioned to him that I had a business. Did he know I did the ghost tours? No, as far as he knew, I was a junior legal aide. Was he the person I saw running through the trees behind the cemetery? Maybe there was more to him than meets the eye. Well, that was a bit creepy. I shook my head, trying to put it all aside.

CHAPTER TWENTY-SIX

THE NEXT DAY Maggie called me, "I got it!" She sounded so excited.

"I assume you're talking about Priscilla's job application?"

"Yes!" She practically screamed into the phone to me.

"Geez, can you say excited?" I laughed.

"Well, playing detective is not something I usually do. Maybe I'll branch out into a new career. A florist detective." She laughed.

I heard another voice in the background. "Did someone say detective?"

It was a man's voice. I listened while Maggie started stammering. "Oh, hello, Detective Mason, I didn't hear you come in." She could barely get that sentence out.

"Am I interrupting anything, something you are investigating?" he asked.

"Oh, no, of course not."

"I'll call you back." And she hung up on me.

I laughed to myself, thinking of her trying to talk herself out of that one.

At the florist shop, Maggie asked, "What can I do for you, detective?"

"I needed to order a plant or a flower arrangement and I'm not sure which she will prefer."

"She? Maybe you can give me an idea of who this is for and I'll let you know what I have and of course, we can always wire an order."

"This is actually for my mom. It's her birthday and her favorite color is yellow, if that helps at all."

"Does she have a preference, maybe roses? Or how does an arrangement of mixed flowers sound?"

"Let's do a mixed arrangement. I just want to make sure it's pretty and preferably will last awhile."

"No problem, I can get this taken care of for you."

They finished up their business and the detective left the shop.

As he was leaving the shop, he turned back to Maggie. "Okay Maggie, you be careful in your new job as a detective and tell your cohort to mind her own business."

Maggie could feel her face redden as he left.

She didn't have time to call Emily back, because who should come walking in but Priscilla.

"Hey," Priscilla said, "What was Detective Mason doing here?"

"Oh, do you know him?"

"Not personally, I just know who he is."

Maggie wondered if Detective Mason had called Priscilla into the station to discuss her meeting with Simon at the Three Pines. The phone rang and that was the end of their conversation.

They were busy for several more hours. Maggie finally had to come to terms with the fact she couldn't talk to Emily again until the shop closed and she was home.

Emily opened her front door that night before Maggie even knocked.

"You didn't call me back," Emily said.

Maggie reached into her purse and pulled out the papers, a job application, and a resume. "Here you go," Maggie said, handing it over. "Sorry I couldn't get back to you, we got busy."

Maggie relayed the conversation she had with Detective Mason.

"Oh my," I grinned. "I would have given anything to have heard you explain your way out of that detective florist comment."

"I did some fast talking, that's for sure. And then after he left, Priscilla came walking in."

Maggie continued, "Priscilla did ask about what Detective Mason was in the shop for. And I asked if she knew him. She said no, but I wonder if he called her into the station to talk about Simon. She just said she knew who he was."

"So, what was Detective Mason doing in the shop?" I asked.

She gave me one of those looks, "Ordering flowers, of course."

I pressed my lips together, "I meant who was he ordering flowers for?"

"Why Emily, what do you think I am, the town gossip?"

I giggled, "I would never say that. Although you do seem to know what's going on and who's doing what."

"He ordered flowers." She smiled, "For his mother. It's her birthday," she admitted. "What a good son he is." She was giving me a sly look. "And he also said for you to mind your own business. That is if he was assuming you were my cohort."

I chose to ignore his comment. "Thanks for bringing this by. I've been on pins and needles all day, since our call."

"I really wanted to call you back, just never had a spare moment when Priscilla wasn't around. I'm going to go on home, I'm beat, but you do your thing. Find out what you can and let me know what you discover, okay?"

I walked her to the door and waved goodbye as she drove off. Then I started reading Priscilla's job application. It only had her current local address, but it did have a listing for her education and prior employers.

I couldn't do an actual background check without her permission, but I'd see what I could find out. And I couldn't call to verify her employment or college degree tonight. I'd have to wait until the morning.

I woke up early the next morning and brewed myself a nice big cup of coffee, added my favorite caramel creamer, and started in. I contacted her former employer and asked to confirm her employment. The HR department confirmed her employment on her last job and the same with the job before that too. I even confirmed her college degree through the school's registrar. Well, that didn't take very long, I thought to myself. She seemed like a pretty straight shooter. Everything seemed to be in order. Guess she really was who she said she was. I'd stop by the shop later on today to let Maggie know.

CHAPTER TWENTY-SEVEN

I BUSIED myself around the house that day, unpacking a couple of boxes that I had previously stored in a closet. They contained old photo albums that my mother had lovingly filled with photos over the years. I proceeded to line them up on my newly refinished bookshelves. Maggie, of course, had helped me with the staining of the shelves and the low glass front cabinets that separated the living room from the dining room.

I emptied both boxes and stepped back to admire my handiwork when I noticed the car parked out front just a little way down the road. I felt my anger rising and I stormed out the door, ready for a confrontation. The concrete walk was cold on my bare feet, but that didn't stop me. It was obvious that the driver had spotted me, because the car engine started and it took off down the road. I caught a slight glance of a man in the car. I thought I recognized the driver. I turned to go back inside, feeling very wary.

I got ready and decided I'd go see a friendly face for a late lunch; of course, that meant paying a visit to The Little Copper Cafe. I had learned to go for a late lunch, that way I could have some uninterrupted visit time with my friend. Claudette greeted me with a warm hello when I entered. I walked over to an empty table and she came over when she was free.

"Hey, I was just thinking about you. You hadn't been in to see me lately."

I laughed, "And I'm way overdue for some of your baked goods."

"So what can I get for you?

"How about a cheeseburger and fries?"

"You got it. I'll bring you back some coffee in just a bit too."

By the time I was halfway through my cheeseburger, Claudette went to lock the door. Finally, I thought, now we have time for a proper chat. "Want to pull up a chair and visit a bit?" I called out to her.

"Sure, let me get some coffee and I'll be right there." She brought over the pot of coffee and an empty cup for herself.

"So, what's new?" she asked when she was all settled. "Any news about Simon's murder?"

She could certainly be direct. "I was wondering what you could tell me about Mr. Richards."

"James Richards?" Claudette asked in between sips of coffee.

"Yes, that's the one."

"Salt of the earth. That's what I can tell you." She was off and running and I felt like I would have to listen hard to keep up. "This foolishness about him stealing money and illegal gambling, well, it's just not so." She had started to take a sip of her coffee, but put her cup back down rather firmly, splashing a little bit out on the tabletop.

"He has been a pillar in this community, been in business here for more than thirty years. He supports a lot of charities and there is absolutely no way he is guilty of those charges. Let me tell you, that young guy he hired, well, I could tell he was nothing but trouble. I tried to warn James, but he was offering a hand up, trying to help this kid turn his life around and what did he get for it?" Claudette paused to take a breath, "He got a boatload of trouble, that's what he got."

Her voice got a little quieter, but still held the same conviction. "You didn't know my husband; his name was Henry and he died almost ten years ago, God rest his soul. Anyway, James stepped up and helped me sort out all my finances and made it so I could open this cafe. He's not a criminal. We've talked and I know he's down. He feels like the town has abandoned him. I suppose it's times like these when you find out who your real friends are."

I decided to tell Claudette about my visit to Mr. Richards and filled her in on the details.

"Well, I'll give you points for originality, but personally I think you have the wrong suspect."

"He got my home phone number and I'm not sure how he got it."

"Oh, my goodness. I am so sorry, I think he got that from me. You see, he called me the other day, rather upset. I don't leave the cafe too often during the day, but I took a quick run over and took him some muffins. Anyway, he described a visit from a junior legal aide. He said he was rather rude by the end of the visit and wanted to apologize to the aide. He told me he called his lawyer, but they didn't have anyone on staff that fit the description of the woman who paid him a visit. Well, one thing led to another and I figured out who had visited him. I'm so sorry, Emily, I started to call you when I got back here to give you a heads up and then I had some trouble in the kitchen and had to hang up. After that I got busy and totally forgot to call you back. Please forgive me. This is how much I trust him. I knew there was no danger in giving out your number."

I was a little hesitant, but I knew Claudette would never knowingly put me in danger. But, I didn't have the same faith in Mr. Richards as she did.

CHAPTER TWENTY-EIGHT

I LEFT the cafe and stopped by to see Maggie; I knew she was waiting for an update.

"Hey there," I said, glancing around as I entered her shop.

"Hi, so what did you find out?" Maggie asked. "We're alone."

"About Priscilla? Nothing, that's what I found out, but I did find out some interesting info about Mr. Richards," I said, following her around the shop. She was pulling various flowers for a new arrangement.

"Ooh, those sunflowers are pretty," I said.

"Focus, Emily, what did you find out about Mr. Richards?"

"He's been parked outside my house on a few occasions. He figured out, with help from Claudette, that I was the one who interviewed him and he has been sitting outside my house. He seems to think I am in danger from whoever actually killed Simon.

"Wow. I don't know him well, but I do have my doubts about the accusations. My grandfather says there is no way he's guilty. So, if we take Mr. Richards out of the picture, what do we know?"

"We know Simon is dead. We thought he was hit over the head and killed, but that's not exactly right either. We know that he was in an unhappy marriage. We know Dara made comments about hitting him upside the head. We know she had seen a divorce attorney."

"Oh, I just heard that Dara was actually at a charity meeting for the hospital on the night Simon died."

"And how did you just happen to hear this?" I looked at her with probably what was an impatient look on my face.

"I made a delivery to the hospital earlier this morning and ran into someone who coordinates their charity auction. She mentioned Dara's work with them and commented that it was a shame about what had happened to Simon. Sorry, I just hadn't gotten around to telling you yet."

"We know Jillian would probably not have advanced at the paper with Simon still there. But honestly, she is so young and very emotional the times that I've seen her. I just don't think she is capable of committing murder."

"I agree with you there," Maggie said, pulling some cobalt blue delphiniums out of the case and adding them to her collection.

"We know Simon had received threats since the story broke about Mr. Richards. We know someone left a threatening note on my doorstep. And we know Priscilla was with him at the Three Pines the night he died and lied about it. Her resume may be clean, but she also lied about knowing Alan too. So, if it wasn't Dara, and Claudette is vouching so much for Mr. Richards, then that just leaves..."

About that time, we heard the old wooden floors creak. We both turned at the sound. Priscilla was standing in the archway connecting the front and back rooms of the shop. She must have come in the back door while we were talking.

"Then that just leaves me." Her eyes were cold and the look on her face was full of contempt. We froze right where we were, staring at her.

She reached into her bag, pulling out a gun, and pointed it at us.

"You think you're so smart. Well, let me tell you what you don't know about Simon. He was my half-brother. I tracked him down through our father. Our dead father. Seems like our father has some bucks," she sneered. "Since Simon never wanted anything to do with him when he was alive, I figured I'd make sure Simon wouldn't have anything to do with his money now that he's dead."

"My knowledge of plants has come in handy. A little conium maculatum in his drink at the Three Pines was all it took. Maggie, you probably know what that is, but Emily, do you?"

I was trying to think quickly, but I had no clue what that was, except I knew it wasn't good. Priscilla had the gun trained directly on me now and took a slow step in my direction. Out of the corner of my eye, I saw Maggie as she slowly crept back toward the counter, seemingly unnoticed by Priscilla.

"Hemlock, that's what it is." Priscilla's voice, which was initially contemptuous now became almost emotionless and matter of fact. "It's relatively fast-acting. With my knowledge of plants, I could make my very own particularly lethal concentrate. Just a little in his drink when he wasn't looking was all it took. I could get rid of Simon and then everything would be mine. Hemlock affects the nervous system, you know, and by the time he left the Three Pines, he was beginning to feel the effects. I followed him when he left and he was having trouble walking. He took the trail behind the cemetery and down the hill, guess he thought that would have been a shortcut to his house. By the time he got to the top of the hill, he fell. I watched him roll down the hill; hitting his head on that boulder at the bottom. I knew if the blow to the head hadn't killed him, he would soon have trouble breathing."

I gasped. Priscilla kept on talking, "I've seen you coming out of the police station, I knew you suspected me, and yes, I was the one who left that note for you. Too bad you didn't pay more attention to it." Now she was pointing the gun at Maggie, "that detective was in here yesterday."

Suddenly the front and back doors burst open. The police rushed in, including Detective Mason. "Drop your weapon," they all yelled. Maggie and I ducked down behind the counter. It was very chaotic for a few seconds, but Priscilla gave up without a fight. They handcuffed her and took her away.

I turned to look at Maggie. "Are you ok?" I asked shakily. We clung to each other, crushing some of the flowers that she still held. I looked at Detective Mason, "How did you happen to show up?"

He smiled, "It was Maggie. She tripped her silent alarm," he said calmly. "Are you ladies ok?"

We were both still shaking from the adrenaline, "I need a nice cup of tea or something stronger to calm my nerves."

"If you can," he said, "we'll need you both to come down to the station to give a statement."

"Yes, we can do that," I ventured, looking at Maggie. "You good?"

"Of course, piece of cake." She was trying to project a brave front, but I could see her hands still shaking.

CHAPTER TWENTY-NINE

MAGGIE and I went to the police station together and gave our statements. I felt exhausted and at the same time thrilled to know Simon's murderer had been arrested.

We left the station together and walked back down to Maggie's shop. Looking around she said, "I think I'm going to get this arrangement together and close up early today."

"You deserve some time off, that's for sure." I agreed. "I'm sorry you got wrapped up in the middle of this."

"What's life without a little excitement," she sighed. "But for future reference," she said pointing a finger at me, "I'll take my excitement in, I don't know, maybe the form of shopping for new shoes and finding out the store is having a ninety-five percent off sale."

"Would those be running shoes, by any chance?"

Maggie laughed out loud, "Oh heck, no. Heels, now that's what I'm talking about."

"Now you're trying to kill me too!" I said in mock alarm. "I'm going home now, before you make me go shopping or something. Want to meet for dinner tonight?"

"I'd love too. I'm going to need some dessert tonight."

I left her shop and headed home, anticipating a long relaxing soak in my tub, to help me shake off the traumatic events of the day.

Later that evening, I grabbed my purse and jacket to go meet Maggie for dinner. I was halfway out the door when my phone rang. I stopped to answer it and recognized the voice of Mr. Richards.

"Why, hello," I said.

"Listen, if you have a moment, I wanted to explain and apologize to you Emily," Mr. Richards began, "The way Claudette spoke of you made me certain you are someone special to her. And from the questions you asked me, I could tell you were investigating Simon's death. I knew I needed to try to keep you safe. I followed you around a little before you realized it, but again I sure didn't mean to frighten you. Please forgive me."

"I appreciate your thoughtfulness, Mr. Richards. Maybe next time you could just be straightforward and let me know what you were doing."

He laughed, "And what would you have said to that?"

"Well, you got me there." I had to agree with him. I never would have approved of him following me around.

"I won't keep you, I just wanted to explain. Good night."

"Good night, Mr. Richards," I said hanging up the phone.

Maggie was waiting for me when I got to the Three Pines. We had decided we deserved to treat ourselves that evening. We got a table and perused the menu.

"I'm thinking about the maple pecan pork chops with the roasted potatoes. What are you getting?" I asked Maggie.

"Oh, that sounds yummy. I think I'll get that," she paused, "and a to-go container, so I can enjoy my dessert."

We ordered our food and enjoyed some cheesy bread while we waited for our meal.

"Is it my imagination or does it look like we have some people staring at us?" I asked, taking a sip of my drink.

Maggie took a quick glance around. "Nope, it's not your imagination at all."

About that time another waitress approached our table. "Hello ladies, I'm sorry to interrupt, but do you remember me?"

"Of course we do. You were the one to let us know that Priscilla and Simon had been in here together the night he died."

"So, is it true? Priscilla was arrested in your shop?" she asked, turning to Maggie.

It seemed like the news of Priscilla's arrest was spreading fast. I suppose that's the way things were in a small town.

"Yes, it's true," we confirmed.

"Wow," she sighed. "Who would have thought she was capable of something like that?" She stood there shaking her head. "I'm sorry. I won't intrude on you anymore. Enjoy your dinner."

Our waitress walked up in a bit with our dinner and we were left to enjoy our evening. We were celebrating. Celebrating the fact that we hadn't been killed that afternoon.

"You were the hero, you know," I said to Maggie. "I didn't know you had an alarm system."

"I had it installed a while back. Sometimes when it's busy, I'll do a little work in the evenings and I just didn't feel comfortable there sometimes by myself; we have a lot more strangers in town these days, and it lowered my insurance as well."

"Well, I'm really glad you had it put in. It definitely paid for itself today."

"Definitely!" Maggie confirmed.

Our waitress stopped by to check on us shortly after we finished our dinner. "So, ladies, will there be dessert tonight?"

"Of course," Maggie said, "we need it after the day we've had."

She brought us the dessert menu and Maggie chose the chocolate chip cookie dough cheesecake and after much consideration, I finally settled on a slice of their decadent peanut butter chocolate cake cheesecake.

I laughed when the pieces arrived. They were definitely larger than normal. "I heard about your day. Enjoy."

I took the first bite of the cheesecake, closed my eyes and savored the flavors.

Maggie laughed at me, "You're going to go into a chocolate and peanut butter coma if you eat all of that."

"Ha! I could say the same thing about you and that oversized piece you have there." I said looking at her generous slice of chocolate chip goodness.

"Yes, but what a way to go."

We laughed, toasted with our coffee. "Here's to good friends and good food."

Maggie laughed and added, "And maybe a little less excitement with our adventures in the future."

NOTES FROM THE AUTHOR

Thank you so much for reading my first Cozy Mystery. My hope is that you will stick with me throughout the series. I have enjoyed writing these stories and watching my characters develop over the course of these books. I hope you enjoy them.

Other books in the series include:
    Murder on the Mountain
    Murder in the Square
    Murder Down the Stairs
    Murder on the Stage
    Murder Down the Aisle

If you would like to receive my newsletter and get information on future books, please go to my website at www. amygrundy.com

Again, thank you for reading this book, I sincerely hope you enjoyed it. Here is a preview of Book Two in this series:

PREVIEW OF BOOK 2 - MURDER ON THE MOUNTAIN

Chapter 1

"Good morning, Emily." I heard a familiar voice and looked around, setting down my coffee cup.

Mrs. Smithers approached my table. She was an elderly lady, with lovely white hair, impeccably applied makeup and large colorful glasses hanging around her neck. A long-time resident of Copper Ridge, Mrs. Smithers managed the town's historical society. She had previously helped me obtain information about the town and some local ghost stories too.

"Hey, good morning, Mrs. Smithers," I said, smiling. "Won't you have a seat?"

I was having breakfast at my favorite spot, The Little Copper Cafe, enjoying some sourdough French toast and crispy bacon.

"No dear, thank you though. I am just picking up a lemon poppy seed muffin before I head over to work. You know I absolutely love the muffins Claudette bakes, and if you haven't tried it, the coffee cake is scrumptious. Oh, but back to business, I wanted to ask you to stop by and see me sometime at the courthouse. I have an intriguing new story for you that I think you could use for your ghost tours." Her lively blue eyes gleamed as she smiled at me mischievously. She knew I was hooked.

"Of course. I'd love to stop by. How about after I finish up here?"

"Perfect, I'll see you soon." She turned and went to pick up her muffin from Claudette and left with a smile on her face.

Claudette, the owner of the cafe, came over and refilled my coffee cup. "Hey, how are you enjoying that French toast?" Claudette was cheery and outgoing. She was one of the first people to welcome me when I moved into town. She had soft brown hair, warm brown eyes, and just the beginnings of laugh lines around her eyes. She reminded me a lot of my mother, maybe not so much with her looks, but with her personality.

She knew I loved my carbs. "You know I never met a carb I didn't like," I laughed. "This French toast is amazing; any chance you'll give me your recipe?"

"I could, but you know if I did, you might quit coming in here to see me."

"That would never happen. Breakfast always tastes better whenever someone else cooks it for me," I laughed. "Mrs. Smithers appears to love your lemon poppy seed muffins."

"It's a new recipe, I'm glad she likes it. Seems like it's going to be popular with my customers. Speaking of which, let me get back to work and I'll leave you to get back to your breakfast before it gets cold." Claudette went on, working her way from table to table, chatting and help her other customers. The Little Copper Café was quite popular in town, and for good reason.

I finished eating my breakfast, paid my check and headed out the door to see Mrs. Smithers. I couldn't help but wonder what she would have for me today.

Chapter 2

Mrs. Smithers had helped me a several months ago when I was starting up my business of giving ghost tours here in Copper Ridge. I was excited to hear what new story she had for me. I zipped up my hoodie as the chilly autumn wind began to blow. This was my favorite time of year with the leaves of the aspen and maple trees turning vibrant shades of yellow, orange and red. I left my car at the cafe, walked across the town square and climbed the courthouse steps. Built in the 1800s, the building had limestone block walls, accented with red sandstone, capped with domes, and an intricate clock tower.

Mrs. Smithers looked up from her reading when I walked in.

"Lovely to see you, my dear." She greeted me as she closed her book. "Let me show you what I found. I think you're going to like it!"

I watched as she opened a cabinet, and pulled out a small worn rectangular wooden box. She handed me a pair of soft white gloves, and pulled out a pair for herself as well. As I pulled my gloves on, I couldn't help but get excited. Whatever she had was obviously very old. She lifted the lid and unwrapped what looked like some sort of diary or logbook. The cover was stained, its edges battered, and she turned the old, yellowed pages very carefully.

"I found this book while looking through some information from the mine. This is a logbook that was kept by the mine manager. He kept track of many things; this one dealt with information regarding his employees. It was rather ordinary reading until I came across this section." She turned the book around and pointed.

I started reading where she indicated. "*Some of the men gave reports of witnessing lights in the woods evening last. They describe them as orbs, green or yellow in color, that appear to float, never landing on the ground. They report walking into the woods but the lights disappear and they are never able to come upon them. The men who have reported seeing these strange lights are some of my most reliable. They are not prone to drunkenness or other such indications of poor character. I am uncertain of what to make of their reports whether they are credible or folly.*"

I looked up at Mrs. Smithers. "What do you think this means?"

"Keep reading, look at this entry over here." She pointed to another page.

"*The men reported seeing the strange lights again. They say they are a sign. Others say they are a bad omen. Every time they are sighted, an accident occurs. The lights were spotted last night and today two men were injured when a support beam collapsed. Mining is far from safe work but I do not believe in the correlation. Neither myself nor my crew chief put stock in such notions. I do not want a few men spreading wild tales and causing disruption among the crew.*"

"That is interesting. Do you have any information about the lights? I wonder what it was they were seeing?"

"Well, that's the interesting thing. We don't know. I suppose he wanted to keep the stories quiet. The miners themselves didn't keep journals, or if they did, we don't have any of them. After the mine closed, there was no reason for the mining camp to remain open, so it closed down. No one lived on the mountain and the story of the strange lights was forgotten. I am going to keep looking to see what else I can find out though," Mrs. Smithers said, closing the book.

"You're right, I can see why you thought this would make a good ghost story. I can use this." I stood there for a moment thinking about what she had just shown me. "Do you have a location for these supposed lights? I'd love to go up the mountain and see what I can find."

"Well I can give you a location to the old mine, but right now that's the best I can do." Mrs. Smithers pulled out a map of the mountain and the surrounding area. "Here is the old mine property," she said, marking the location. "What we don't know for certain is what direction the miners were looking in, in relation to their camp. I'll keep looking through our records here and see what else I can find. Why don't you take this map with you and if I find anything else I'll let you know. This is so exciting. I love a good mystery."

"By any chance are these the same lights people have reported seeing in the old cemetery?" I asked her.

"People around here have said those could be miners with their lamps searching for lost fellow miners. These lights could be the same, we just don't know. They've had accidents at the mine, of course, some worse than others. Sometimes a miner would make it out and later die from their injuries. Those men are the ones who are buried in the old cemetery. But then they had that big collapse, and those miners' bodies were never recovered. From what I've read, they considered closing the mine due to the lack of ore being recovered. Anyway, after the last big collapse, well that was it. They closed it down for good."

"Wow, that's quite the story. Those were some rough times. I can't imagine what it must have been like to be a miner or to live in those days. I suppose I'm way too used to my modern conveniences," I admitted.

"Yes, I suppose they were. Times have changed so much here in Copper Ridge, even since I was born."

I smiled at her, "I'll bet you have some stories to tell. Listen, I want you to know I really appreciate all the information you dig up for me. Thank you so much for taking the time to do the research and letting me know about what you find."

"Well, dear, I love researching, I've just never had anyone to share it with. You have made me feel young again."

"We make quite the pair, don't we?" I reached out and gave her a quick hug. She was such a sweet, endearing lady. "Would you care to take a drive up the mountain with me?"

"Well, I'd love to, my dear. It sounds like quite the adventure."

We scheduled our jaunt up the mountain for a day later in the week when the historical society was closed.

I watched as she wrapped the old journal and put it away. "I'd better be going. I've got errands to run today. Thanks again for the new info though. I really appreciate it."

"Oh, anytime my dear, anytime."

I left my white gloves on the counter, "Good-bye. Have a good day."

"You too, my dear."

I left the courthouse and was hit with a chilly gust of wind. I loved the mountains and I loved the fall. It just made me feel alive. I got my car and headed off to get some shopping done and couldn't help but look up at the mountain. I laughed to myself, no lights to be seen now, but of course it was daytime.

Chapter 3

I finished running my errands and had plenty of time to get ready before I headed out to meet Maggie. She and I had agreed to meet for dinner that evening. Maggie, Copper Ridge's local florist was a good friend whom I had met shortly after moving to town. We were both about the same age. She had a chin-length blonde bob with lots of golden highlights, while I had long dark red hair. We met in local coffee shop, when she literally bumped into me spilling iced latte all over my clothes. We started chatting and before I knew it, Maggie was at my house, helping me renovate my little Craftsman bungalow. We enjoyed spending time together and had hit it off right from the start. Tonight, I drove back into town to meet her at her house; it was her turn to cook. Her home was located in the top floors above her flower shop, Maggie's Creations, right off the town square. She had done a lot of the work herself, making it into an open concept downstairs and bedrooms upstairs. She had kept the exposed brick walls, refinish the old hardwood floors, and replaced the old glass in the arched windows. I had given her grief about living so close to her work, thinking it would be nice to get away from work and go home, but then I saw the place and knew why she loved it.

The fragrance of good home cooking met me before she even opened her door. Maggie greeted me with, "I hope you are hungry."

"Oh, my goodness, it smells wonderful in here," I said, dropping my jacket over the back of the couch.

"I made us some good old-fashioned comfort food tonight. When the weather turns chilly, I like to indulge myself. How does homemade chicken pot pie sound?"

"It sounds absolutely wonderful, and look at that crust." My mouth watered as I looked at the golden flaky crust. We served our plates and sat down to eat. Things had started to quiet down in town following the murder of our town's lead newspaper reporter, Simon Wilson. Copper Ridge was a small town of approximately eight thousand or so and was situated at the base of Angel Mountain. The town had most recently re-invented itself and made most of its income from tourism. We had mountains in the area for hiking and camping, a river running through town for rafting, along with a fair number of artisans and craftsmen who had come to town, opening shops mostly around the old town square. I was a recent newcomer to town myself following the death of my mother. She had left me with a modest inheritance and I had started a business giving ghost tours. The town was full of old historic sites which I used as stops on my tour.

"Maggie, this is so good. You'll have to show me how to make a crust like this," I laughed. "Or better yet, I'll just let you cook dinner for me more often."

"Not on your life," She laughed.

"So, what's new?" I asked, sipping my coffee.

"By any chance do you want to make a trip up the mountain with me, maybe this weekend?" Maggie asked

"Sure." I looked up, curious that the mountain had come up twice in conversations now. "But why are we going up there?" Besides the old abandoned mine, most of the mountain was heavily wooded and not very developed. There were some private cabins dotted about for seasonal guests and rough hiking trails, some streams for fishing, but not much else.

"Several years ago, an elderly gentleman came into the shop. Seems his wife was dying and he had me order multiple kinds of orchids for delivery to their home, some quite exotic. He lived in a gated estate about thirty miles from here. It wasn't a huge house, but he did have a good bit of property, with some lovely gardens from what I saw. Anyway, seemed like orchids were her favorite. So, for the last weeks of her life, he surrounded her with them. He had us making trips to their home several times a week, bringing in more and more of them. He loved her so much." Maggie's voice got a little quieter. "Then she died." From the look on her face I knew she was remembering her customer during that tragic time. "He was so sad and very distraught. He gave me very specific instructions regarding the kind of flowers he wanted for her funeral. I made sure they were perfect, and just what he wanted. He was such a sweet old guy. Anyway, after the funeral, I didn't see or hear from him anymore. Recently though, his attorney stopped by the shop. Seems like the old gentleman has also now passed away and he left me some land up on the mountain. I thought I'd go up there and take a look."

"Wow. Those must have been some special flowers."

"I think he was lonely and so appreciative of the care and attention we showed him and his wife. I tried my best to be as exact as possible, always getting specifically what he wanted."

"You were what he needed, at a time when he needed it the most."

"Well, I was just glad to be able to be there for him, even if it was just to deliver the flowers. I would never have expected anything in return, much less have something left to me in a will." Maggie replied.

"Well, let's go check it out. I really wanted to go up there anyway. Mrs. Smithers and I were talking this morning. It seems like back when the mine was open, there were reports of some of the miners seeing unexplained lights off in the woods. The miners tried to follow the lights through the forest, but the lights would just vanish. The information Mrs. Smither's showed me said the miners thought the lights were a bad omen. So, she and I plan to drive up the mountain to the old mine and have a look around."

"It's settled then. Why don't you let her know what time to meet and we'll go see my property and look for those lights." Maggie glanced over at my empty plate. "Want some more?"

"No, I'm good. That was really delicious." Maggie took my plate and walked off to the kitchen. "Promise me, you'll make that again sometime."

Are you ready for dessert?" She called out from the kitchen.

"Dessert? Maybe you should have said there would be dessert; I might have stopped eating sooner."

"Oh, don't give me that, you know you have room for dessert." Maggie knew I'd probably have to be dying to pass up a dessert.

And then she brought it to the table. Lava brownies baked in little iron skillets and now topped with vanilla ice cream and extra hot fudge. "Ta-da!"

I cut into that chocolate brownie and the warm, rich, creamy chocolate center oozed out, mixing with my melting ice cream. "Oh, I think I've died and gone to chocolate heaven."

We chatted more and before you knew it, we were both

scraping the chocolate remains from our dishes. "I think I'm going to explode, but what a way to go."

We washed the dishes together, then firmed up our plans for the weekend.

"Thanks for dinner, next time it'll be my turn to cook," I promised. See you this weekend."

As I made my way downstairs to my car, I couldn't help but glance up at the mountain. Of course, I didn't see any dots of light up there now, all was dark. I couldn't help but wonder how many cabins were up there and if anyone up there had ever seen lights or anything else out of the ordinary. What had the miners actually seen?

ABOUT THE AUTHOR

Hello readers.

My name is Amy and I'm the author of the Copper Ridge Mystery series. I'd like to say I've had a passion for writing my whole life, but that would be untrue. My husband of forty plus years encouraged me to try my hand at writing cozy mysteries in the spring of 2019 and I LOVE IT!

A former nurse, I live in the Houston area. I enjoy a quiet life with my husband, children, and grandchildren. My family also includes one lovable dog and five very independent cats. When I'm not writing I enjoy running marathons with support from my friends at Ft. Bend Fit, jigsaw puzzles and always a good cup of coffee.

I hope you will enjoy my Copper Ridge Mystery series and thank you for your support.